CILLIAN
&
KAT

USA TODAY BESTSELLING AUTHOR

From *USA Today* and the *Wall Street Journal* best-selling author Willow Winters, comes a sexy second-chance MC romance.

I took the fall for a crime I didn't commit, and it cost me everything. Including the only woman I ever loved.

I'm not the man she fell in love with.
Four years behind bars made me harder, colder … with a temper I can't control.

But then I look at her and nothing else matters.
I'm broken without her and a shell of the person I used to be.

She is my one and only. My addiction and my sanity.
I could never imagine how time would change everything and how far we'd drift apart … but she can't deny this tension and she can't hide the way her body reacts to mine.

She was mine once and nothing can ever change that.

I only hope the secrets of the past four years don't tear us apart the moment I make her mine again.

SEXY
AS SIN

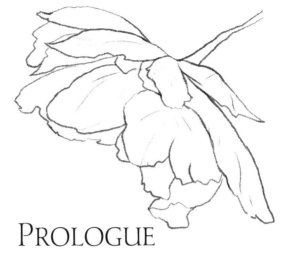

PROLOGUE

KAT

If I had known what was going to happen ... I would have begged him not to go. I would have even fought him to keep us from walking through those doors. That's the thing about fate, though—you're never given a heads-up. But I should have known because everything was just right. When everything is perfect, it's eventually all going to crumble and there's not a damn thing you can do to stop it.

FOUR YEARS AGO

As my heels click against the cement stairs and I walk into the garage, I note that it feels like home. I know every square inch of this place. I've practically grown up inside of these four walls. With an arm wrapped around my waist and the bite of the night chill outside waning, all I can do is let a smile slip into place.

Everything is familiar, from the smell of the oil that's ever present to all the mechanic tools hung neatly on the walls. Any item you could ever need to repair or build a motorcycle is here. Hell, I don't care in the least about the work that's done here, yet I bet I could name most of the tools, just from Cill asking me to hand them to him over the years. At a glance I could tell if any of them were out of order—that's how much time I've spent here. Hours and days and years. Basically my whole life. It may seem strange to other people, but the rumble of bikes paired with the loud laughter and hollering that come with the men who are always here is my kind of heaven. I bet ordinary people feel like this when they walk into a cozy living room.

My leather jacket presses against Cillian's leathers with a faint squeak as we squeeze by the narrow opening to the rest of the three-story building.

The best part by far is holding Cillian's hand, just like I've done for years. His fingers loop easily through mine like we're meant to be together. We *are* meant to be together.

I can't remember a time when I didn't have a crush on him. In high school we started dating with approval from both of our fathers. My heart warms to think about him as my high school sweetheart. My father said it would make sense; his father said it was a business decision done right. Mob connections from my father, MC from his.

I'm head over heels for the boy I've always been told I'm meant to be with. Now that we're older, it's only gotten more intense.

An hour ago, we were in his bed. With his hard body pressed against mine and a cold sweat slipping across my sensitized skin, I cried out his name and he murmured his love for me in the crook of my neck.

Cillian's tall, with hard but lean muscles that work against me. I just barely come up to his shoulders. I don't think anyone could imagine a man like him saying the sweet things he does to me when he comes, whispering his adoration and promises for our future. It's like he's showing me some secret part of him that no one else will ever get to see. I hold that secret close while we walk into the garage together. He pulls me tighter as we move through the door to the staircase at the side of the building.

One thing everyone does know: he's my ride or die and I'm his, and we're both protected in every way imaginable.

With the rec room on the second floor only a threshold away, he bends down and kisses me. "I wish I could take you back to bed," he murmurs, his voice throaty and laced with sin and sex appeal.

A shiver runs through my body and travels lower, bringing

a blush to my cheeks.

"You should," I tease him, nipping his bottom lip. I'd fuck him all night, every night. On more than one occasion we've fooled around till dawn. Nothing is better. He knows my body, every inch of it and every secret. Cillian's my first, and I don't want any other men.

"You want to turn back then and not go to Sunday dinner?"

"Yeah," I say and capture my bottom lip between my teeth before adding playfully, "Let's go before anyone sees us." Tugging on his hand is useless and I already know it's not going to happen.

Every Sunday, we have to be here for dinner. No exceptions. After all, it's both a family and MC occasion.

He laughs and with his gaze lifting past me to the threshold, he seems to consider it. The rough pad of his thumb glides along the stubble on his chin before he looks back down at me, a wanting look I know well in his light blue gaze. "They'd wonder where we went. They'd talk about us."

"Who cares?" I slip my arms under his leathers and tug at the fabric, making my desire known as I slide my fingers up his back. "They already talk about us."

If our fathers weren't in charge, the whispers would be heard far more often. I don't care what people say. I only want Cillian. Everything I dreamed of in high school is right there in his eyes. Our whole future.

"After dinner. I promise," he tells me with a handsome

but cocky grin. "I'll take you back to bed after dinner."

The tip of my nose nudges against his as I let out a small moan of protest; it's nearly a mewl of want. Cill's deep groan as he backs me up to the wall and lowers his lips to mine forces a simper to my lips that grows into a full-blown smile as he kisses down my neck. His rough stubble and roaming hands are everything I want and need.

Just as my head falls back and my breathing turns heavy, Cill backs away and then cracks a smirk at my mouth opening in protest and disbelief.

He chuckles at me and I smack his chest. "After dinner, Hellcat."

Swatting my ass, he keeps me moving and I don't miss a beat, getting on my tiptoes to nip his lower lip.

The guys are already gathering in the rec room and someone must catch a glimpse of us because they call out for Cill. A low groan of annoyance leaves me and Cillian gives me a rough chuckle in response. It's like one big family, and I love that too. One big happy family with Cillian's dad in charge after mine handed him a business deal he couldn't refuse. I don't know exactly what they do, and if I'm honest, I don't want to. Cill says not to worry; my father tells me to do as I'm told and not ask questions. All in all, I'm aware they go out on runs for weeks at a time. When they leave, Cill is anxious and calls me every night. When they come home, he can't keep his hands off me.

He's loyal to me and all Cill's ever asked is for me to stay loyal to him, to trust him and not to worry. I'll take that response over my father's any day.

There's already a crowd in the rec room, the chatter intensifying as we walk in and Reed, his best friend, greets us with a tip of his chin, a smile on his face. He looks like the cat that ate the canary and I wonder what he knows.

My mind slips back to what I thought Cill said last night. I could have sworn he mentioned marriage. It seems silly to be nervous like I am for him to ask, since we both know we're meant to be married. But he hasn't yet and every day that passes by, I know he's going to ask soon. I feel it in the pit of my stomach.

"You want a beer from the back?" Reed questions, gesturing to the other side of the floor.

"Hell yeah," Cill answers and I nod too. I'm only eighteen and Cill's nineteen, but liquor has always flowed easily for us here. Maybe that's another reason I prefer this place to home.

Part of this open space is an expansive kitchen, separated from the rest by a countertop, and there are leather couches, an old coffee table and a professional pool table on the other end. The rack is on the table next to some chalk, but the cues are hung up because no one's playing right now.

A couple of women, two friends I've met a handful of times but I forget their names, sit on the side of the coffee table, leaning forward and talking to Finn and Cill's uncle,

Eamon. It didn't take me long to learn everyone's roles. Finn is the treasurer, which seems at odds with his large stature and weight. He's first generation and formed the club with Eamon and Cill's father decades ago. His accent is thick, as is his Irish temper.

Eamon is the road captain ... but also the enforcer. He's much leaner and again it seems to go against natural thought until you see the man in a ring. Cill's uncle loves to tell stories of "back in the day, when I was a fighter ..."

If another person walked in right now, they might be intimidated. The room is riddled with leather and tattooed skin. Not everyone gets it, but I do. I'm not afraid.

Unlike one of those women, who has a nervous laugh that still hasn't left her. I watch as Finn's brow raises and he leans back. Both he and Eamon are older than the two blondes, one platinum, one dirty blonde, both of them gorgeous. The two men have always had hangers-on and it's never sat right with me. I get that they don't want commitment like the others; they don't want "old ladies." The term makes me roll my eyes. But seeing women come and go is uncomfortable. It's family dinner and if they don't intend on them being family, they shouldn't be here. It's not like it's an intimate gathering. There are over a dozen people here already and another two dozen or so to come. But still ...

I've always found his uncle Eamon a bit disrespectful when it comes to things like that, but as Cill says, they're old school. Which again, makes my eyes roll.

I start to take off my jacket, but a chill blows in and I think better of it, opting to leave it on even though Cill takes his off.

All the windows in the rec room are open. Fresh fall air comes in through the screens. It's early autumn, but already chilly at night. The sun is just starting to set and through the blinds it's easy to see it sinking into the woods behind us.

Nerves settle through me as Cill's hand parts from mine and he has a hushed conversation with Reed. Tonight's the night we're going to tell our fathers our plans for next year. Any other daughter would probably be excited to tell her parents she got a college acceptance letter. My father, though, doesn't like the idea of me leaving and lately he's been kind of off. My mother passed two years ago and he's been downhill ever since, falling into the bottle every night. Part of me feels guilty for leaving, but like Cill said, I have to live my life and I'll show my father it's for the better.

I start college in town next fall, and Cill's happy for me. He's proud, even if he'll be staying with the club. After all, it bears his family name: Cavanaugh Crest. He has to because he's vice president of the Cavanaugh East and this is our home. But we're going to get our own place together halfway from here to State College.

The crack of a beer snaps me out of it and Reed smiles as I look up at him, tipping my head in gratitude.

"Thanks," I say, accepting the drink with a mock cheers and

he and Cill don't miss a beat to continue their conversation. My gaze filters through the room, but I don't see Missy anywhere, Cill's aunt. She's practically his mother since Cill's mom passed when he was just a baby. She's probably out grabbing a few more things for tonight. I'm restless without her here, telling me what I can do to help.

Someone comes down the stairs from the third level, footsteps loud and unselfconscious. It's mostly offices up there on the top floor of the three-story construction and a few bedrooms for people to crash if they need them.

"Kat's going to college," Cillian blurts out to Reed. "She got into the premed program, isn't that fucking amazing?" His fingers slip through mine again and he brings my knuckles to his lips, then kisses them.

My cheeks flush at the compliment, but I don't have much time to react other than to hug Reed back because my phone is ringing.

I hear Reed ask about my father's reaction as I dig out my phone from my pocket. Reed knows how it is, and speak of the devil, my dad's name is on the screen.

He's probably on his way and forgot something or he's running late. He's been late to everything recently.

"Hey, Dad."

"Are you already at the garage?" His voice sounds different than expected, anxious maybe.

"Yes." I huff a laugh at him a little. "Can't you hear it?" It's far too loud in here and it just got louder with Missy yelling out *coming through*, a pan of something in one hand and a bag in the other.

It's too loud to hear what my dad is saying.

I have to drop Cill's hand. I hate letting go of him, but I'll only be gone for a few minutes. He looks down at me and I tilt my head toward the stairwell. He bends to kiss my cheek, his rough stubble grazing against my skin and I catch a hint of his masculine scent that I love. It's woodsy, but fresh like the ocean. Plugging one ear, I make my way through the crowd to the little empty space at the foot of the stairs. Cill watches me go as I try to hear what my father's saying.

Something about going somewhere quiet. No shit, I can hardly hear him.

"Kat." My name is nearly a curse hissed through the phone with impatience.

"Sorry, Dad. I couldn't hear you. Say that again?"

"Did you find your mother's mug?"

My whole body goes cold with a numbing chill. *My mother's mug.* I cross my arms over my chest instinctually, hoping I didn't hear those words. The party is still pretty loud, even in here. Maybe I got it wrong. "What did you say?"

"Did you find your mother's mug?"

The blood drains from my face and it's hard to keep my expression neutral. It's our code phrase. It means I'm in danger.

We made the phrase before my mom died, and just the

mention of her makes my stomach sour. My dad has only used it once before while I was at school. I walked out the front doors without telling anyone and came to the club. Everything was fine and it was only a test. Which I'm hoping he's doing again. Just testing me, even though it would be fucking cruel to do it today.

"I'm already here, Dad." My voice tightens when I realize that it could be he's the one in trouble. Something might have happened to him.

"Is there anyone around you who can hear me?" My gaze lifts and locks with Cill, only a few strides away through the threshold. He mouths to me, "Everything all right?" and I can't answer.

"Kat, answer me," my father demands at the same time that Cill motions for me to come back to him. I slip closer to the chaos that is the rec room but stay just on the other side of the threshold where most of the noise is blocked.

Cill looks down into my eyes, keeping me there as he asks in a hushed tone, "Are you okay?"

All I can do is answer, "No."

My father hears me say it too. "Good," he states over the phone.

I almost correct him to tell him I'm not alone and that Cill may be able to hear, probably everyone else around us too, but Cill takes my phone out of my hand.

His expression turns from concerned to serious in an

instant. He's silent as he raises his hand.

Fear slips down my spine and then over my shoulders, burrowing deeper inside as Cill's expression hardens. Frozen to the core, all I can do is watch. With Cill's hand raised, one by one the room is silenced. One by one their eyes move to the VP and then to me when they realize it's my phone in his hand. The laughter stops. We're surrounded by his uncle and his dad. Their friends. Members of the club. They're all friends with my father too. They were friends growing up and now I grew up here. Cill grew up here. That's how we're part of the MC. We belong here. I tell that to myself over and over again. I belong here. I'm safe here. I am.

I've always been a part of this club, but as the room goes silent and Cill puts the phone on speaker, careful to mute himself first, I feel the walls caving in.

This must be some kind of nightmare.

"The cops are coming," my father says into the dead silence of the room. If I wasn't paralyzed with fear, I'd fall over or run. I can barely swallow, let alone move a limb.

"He says the cops are coming," Cill says, loud enough for everyone to hear.

"Kat. You're going to be safe when the cops come," my dad continues and I wish I could tell my father he's on speaker, but he would want everyone to know too, wouldn't he? If the cops are coming, everyone here should know about it. "Just let them arrest you." My eyes widen in shock and then my mouth drops open. "They're going to let you go, but you're going to be arrested for your protection. You understand me?"

Cill's dad, the head of the MC, the president, the man in charge, reaches in for the phone. As I peek up at him, his gaze is filled with a hate I've never seen from him. My hands tremble and I instinctively take a step back, my shoulders hitting the wall behind me.

It takes Cill wiping my cheek to realize there are tears streaming down my face.

"I don't understand. I don't understand any of this," I barely get out as Cill's father turns his back on us and everyone in the rec room moves at the president's command.

Cill stays in the hall with me, comforting me of all things and as if on cue, the sound of sirens can faintly be heard sneaking in through the open windows.

My heart hammers and I still can't wrap myself around what's just happened.

I know, without my father telling me, there won't be enough time to run. He's giving me this information with only minutes to spare. My dad isn't at the party because he knew this would happen and he didn't want to risk getting arrested.

"He's a rat," I whisper as reality grips me and Cill pulls me in close to his chest. "It's going to be okay," he says. "I've got you."

Oh, God, how could my father do this?

Cill rocks me and kisses my hair, whispering something

but I don't hear it over the pounding of my heart.

It's surreal. This is the moment I know everything has changed and there's no going back.

For four years, I live with this memory. The memory of everything crumbling before my eyes. Even with Cill's arms around me, I knew nothing would ever be the same. I couldn't have imagined what I'd have to live through next. What we'd both have to live through.

Cillian said it would be okay, and I wanted to believe him so badly. He promised he'd help me. He'd make it all right. I stood there trembling as he disappeared into the back of a squad car with his hands cuffed behind his back, the red, white, and blue lights scattered across the pavement.

They thought since he was only nineteen, he'd get a lighter sentence. And he might have, if he'd named names.

But he didn't give up a single person. He took the fall for the club with a sentence of ten years, with the chance of getting out early for good behavior.

My father ran, but I stayed.

And my world changed forever.

CHAPTER 1

KAT

PRESENT TIME

The girl I was at eighteen is long gone. After everything that went down, she's a forgotten memory and the woman I face in the mirror is guarded and reserved ... for good reason.

In the last four years, nearly everyone I've ever known has avoided me at all costs. I suppose I'm lucky to simply be ignored and left on my own. Worse things have happened when crime families excommunicate members. It's partly because I was only eighteen, Lydia told me.

From both of my past families, only one person remained my friend on each side. Lydia, thankfully, told her family to fuck off when they warned her to stay away. No one wants to be associated with a rat. Even if I didn't do it, and it was all my father, I'm guilty by blood.

On the other side, the MC, it was Reed who made sure I was all right … that changed, though, so really I only have Lydia.

Just that thought makes my blood run cold.

"You feeling all right to go in?" Lydia, my best friend since we were itty bitty, pauses outside my house. She dyed her brunette hair a shade darker recently and the moonlight hits it just right, highlighting a bit of red as her fingers toy with the ends. Her gray sweatshirt is a size too big, making her look even smaller than she already does in those worn black skinny jeans.

"Feeling all right to go in?" I echo and her deep brown eyes widen as she looks back at me like I'm crazy.

With my free hand I dig the keys out of my purse, ignoring the uneasy feeling. They're always falling down to the very bottom corner. Almost like they're trying to get out.

"Seriously," Lydia presses, a hand landing on my shoulder as she glances from me to my front door. "Are you sure you're okay to go in?"

"Yeah, it's fine," I say and shrug, fiddling with the keys and then dropping every ounce of fear to move forward regardless.

"I mean, someone broke in, so it's not fine," she says, emphasizing the words *broke in* and waits for me to meet her eyes.

I shrug again. "I try not to let it get to me."

That's the best attitude for moving through life, I've learned. Don't let things get to you or you could worry yourself sick and find yourself crying every hour of every day. Give yourself a few minutes to feel your emotions and get on with it. Keep your chin up.

That's all I could do after everything with the MC fell apart, and it's all I can do now. It's made me a stronger person. Some people might have collapsed under the weight of that life change, and God knows I wanted to, but I didn't. I carried on. Even when my dad vanished into witness protection and left me with nothing, I kept going.

I shift the bouquet of flowers in my left hand to the other one as we go up the steps, keys jingling as we go.

The benefit of working for the florist just outside town is that I get to take leftovers home on Friday. We're closed on Saturdays and Sundays, and my boss lets me have some of the blooms that look like they might not make it through the weekend. Only the freshest flowers for our customers. This bouquet of white peonies will have a happy home in the mason jar that's centered on the hand-me-down table in the small kitchen-dining room combo.

"Well, I'm coming in with you," Lydia says and crosses her arms over her chest as if I'd object.

"Good," I tell her and point the flowers at her, pausing with the keys slipped into the lock of the door, "'cause I have two bottles of red that aren't going to drink themselves."

Lydia cracks a hint of a smile, but she doesn't let up that the break-in isn't something I should make light of.

Swallowing down that thought, I push open the front door and I'm met with the *beep beep beep* of the new alarm system that requires a code I quickly punch in.

The moment I hit the little green button, it's silent save for Lydia pushing the front door shut and letting out a sigh of relief.

"See, safe and sound. The alarm system was a good idea," I tell her as she looks around like she hasn't been here nearly every weekend since I rented out the place.

It's a small house, a little rough around the edges but with good bones. The inheritance my mom left me was supposed to go toward my college tuition, but that fell through. Just like most everything in my life.

"What did the police say?" Lydia asks as we go in and I toss my keys on the kitchen table, then hang my purse over the back of one of the wooden chairs. Setting the flowers down, I follow Lydia's gaze. She scopes out the house like she doesn't trust it, her eyes wandering from room to room.

"You know I didn't call the cops." Lydia stares at me, eyes wide with exasperation. She's silent, though, 'cause she knows that's not something I'd ever do.

Her mouth opens and closes with a silent protest, but then they form a thin line.

"You ready for a glass?" I ask her and she reluctantly nods, slipping her bag off her shoulder and draping it over her chair. "Let me just have a look around," she says without actually asking permission. With my head in the cabinet, snagging two glasses, I listen to the old wooden floors creak as Lydia goes about her way.

I have everything I need here. A little kitchen, a little living room. A bathroom. Two bedrooms. It's plenty of room for me, but barren for the most part.

I can't imagine what anyone would want to steal. Nothing was taken but when I came home, the front door was wide open with the small glass panel busted out, answering the question of how the intruder got in. I'm not going to lie, I was terrified at first.

That's the only reason I called Reed. I had to.

I didn't see anything out of place and he didn't see anything that made me worry. The alarm was his idea, though, and he had it done in a day. Emotions toss and turn as I remember the way he looked at me and how I couldn't even look back at him.

With a long exhale I snatch up my glass of wine in one hand, grab scissors for trimming the flowers in the other, and take both to the table.

I've spent some time putting the place together. I found the dish towel that hangs on the oven at a thrift store last winter. I liked the look of the owl embroidered on the front, with teal streaks running through it and a floral pattern in the background. I hung new curtains just before the break-in happened. They have a bit of blue in the pattern that goes with the dish towel. I have a teal teapot I'm in love with and a thick floor mat by the sink that cushions my feet when I'm washing dishes.

It's cozy and cute and I'm sure whoever broke in was sorely disappointed. If only they'd known I was broke and barely making it by.

"I still wish you'd called the cops," Lydia murmurs as she makes her way back into the kitchen, striding right for her glass of wine.

"I called Reed," I tell her as if it's no big deal, but my attempt at a casual tone is anything but.

"Did they help you at all?"

They. Lydia doesn't say MC, and a chill creeps down my spine. I can't ever think about the club anymore without feeling an empty pit in my stomach. Loss and sadness. They were my family, and I lost almost all of them that night.

"Reed said he'd look into it for me."

"And?"

I shake my head, focusing on tossing the stems of the flowers and not looking her in her eyes. I know there will be questions there and I'm not ready to answer them. "Haven't heard anything."

One of the things I love most about Lydia is that she knows when to push and pry versus when to drink wine with me talking about nothing, pretending like it's all okay.

"You okay otherwise?"

"Yeah." And I really am okay. It took a long time to feel normal after what happened that night four years ago and seeing Reed brought it all back and then some. "Yeah, I'm fine," I tell her and myself both.

It took a long time to stop waking up with tears in the corners of my eyes. I still miss the MC and I never drive down Cedar Lane just to avoid any thoughts of the garage and the club. I think anyone would miss a group of people who were like a family to them. But I don't cry about it anymore. At least not much.

Lydia sighs a little. "You want a snack?"

"You know I do."

"Chips?" She's already digging through my pantry like it's hers too. That's how it's been for most of our lives. She's as comfortable in my kitchen as I am in hers. I could sleep in her bed as easily as I could sleep in mine.

"You know I'm going to miss this," I comment and wish I hadn't. I know she already feels guilty about leaving me here while she takes off, living out her dreams.

"It's not like I'll be gone forever," she chides, the bag of sour cream and onion chips crinkling in her hands.

With an audible inhale, I tell her she better not be.

I center the flowers on my countertop and riffle through the pile of mail, grimacing at the bill I've been avoiding, the one stamped red. "Ah, fuck it, I'll deal with it on Monday." I toss the mail back onto the counter, feeling free of it. Bills can wait for one more day. I want to savor this time with Lydia. It's going to go so fast. "Why do you have to leave me again?"

"College."

"Right, right, right." I grin at her to cover up the ache in my heart. "The whole doing better for yourself and all that," I joke.

I laugh at her and she fake laughs back at me until we're both actually laughing. I'm going to miss her so much. She's been the only constant in my life for so long. But it's what's best for her. She's going to be a doctor one day.

"So ..." The tone of the conversation shifts with that one word and I'm on alert again. I stare her down, but she stares into the red of her glass, her fingers fiddling with the skinny and tall stem. "You feeling okay with Cillian getting out soon?"

My stomach drops at the casual question. I'm frozen with my glass at my lips, ready to take another sip. Finally I do it just so I can complete the movement, then put it back down on the countertop. I don't taste a thing. "I didn't know Cill was getting out. No one told me."

Lydia's dark eyes go wide and then narrow. "But he's staying with you?" She makes the statement almost like it's a question.

"What?"

"That's what Reed said. He couldn't convince him otherwise." My head falls back with disbelief. He was just here. Standing right where she is.

"What?" Pure nerves crush into my stomach. "When did he tell you that?"

"Last week," she answers nervously. "How didn't he tell you?"

"How didn't anyone tell me?" I respond, pushing my wine away.

"Cillian is coming here?" Emotions swarm through me, making every thought harder to focus on.

"I swear to God that's what he said. He came in and—"

"Reed came in?" I interrupt her to clarify and while she's rushing out an explanation of what happened, panic takes over.

All I can see is Cillian, standing in this small rental, taking up every inch of the place and staring back at me with his sharp blue eyes, asking why I stopped coming, why I stopped calling. My body goes cold and I can barely hear a word Lydia says.

You stopped calling too, I can already hear myself answering.

And his imagined answer makes my fingers go numb: *'Cause you stopped loving me, Hellcat.*

"Are you okay?"

"What?" I snap out of it and have to wipe under my eyes.

"I'm so sorry, Kat," Lydia says and rushes over to me but I put a hand up, stopping her.

"I'm fine."

"I should have told you the second Reed said something but I just assumed you didn't bring it up 'cause—"

"I'm fine," I repeat, hardening my voice and she's silenced by it.

"I should have told you."

"Do you know when?" I ask her, not bothering with should haves and could haves.

Staying with me. That means staying here, in this tiny house. The one that's meant to be a bridge away from the past. No one said a word to me. Not Reed. Not Lydia. I had no idea.

"I'm not sure ... soon, though. In order to be released, he needs a place to stay. Reed didn't tell you anything?"

"No." No one told me anything. "Don't I—don't I need to sign something for that?"

"Well, Reed helped you get this place, right?" The chair protests against the floor as she takes her seat again, holding the glass with both hands.

"Yeah." I needed someone to cosign with me. *Fucking Reed.* If he were here, I'd lay into him. How could he do that, knowing what happened?

A voice answers all on its own. If Cill told him to make it happen, he'd do it.

I nearly voice the thought; instead I swallow it down with

another large gulp.

I don't know what to think. I don't know what to say. I feel numb and light-headed, like I might pass out any second. "He's coming home and he didn't tell me. He's coming here and Reed didn't tell me."

"Everyone's been keeping secrets," Lydia murmurs, and she gives me a look full of sorrow before taking a swig. "You want me to stay with you?"

I whisper, "Yeah. Can you just stay 'til I fall asleep?"

"Of course," she answers, reaching out for my hand and I let her take it. A million thoughts overwhelm me. Every single one about Cillian. Every single one, a regret.

Chapter 2

Cillian

The rumble of the bike beneath me almost broke me earlier today, when the sun was setting across the horizon and the pale hues brushed against the barbed wire of the fence I left behind me.

The grip of the handle, the rev of the engine only inches below me and the wind against my face. Four years went by in a blur, yet the life I left behind feels as if I barely know it anymore.

"You sure?" Reed questions as he parks his truck, and the alcohol swirling in my blood makes my head sway.

The idea of being released early on probation was one thing, and the expectations I had for this night were low, but tonight is anything but the celebration the men claimed it to be as beer bottles clinked and they cheered.

Longing for what used to be sunk its claws into me. As I stare at Kat, the light from her kitchen against the dark night giving me every detail, I sink deeper into the worn leather seat of Reed's truck; regret and something else I can't articulate weigh me down.

Who is she now? This woman I used to love and now a woman I don't recognize. Four years and her absence changed what was once between us. I barely remember what we talked about the last time we spoke, but I know she didn't tell me she loved me. Her calls had stopped months before, but I kept calling her.

Until she didn't say those words back. That was over a year ago and yet somehow I thought this would be the right thing to fucking do the night I get out of prison.

"Fuck," I say and my hand runs down my face as I lean my head back, letting the reality sink in.

"You can stay with me," Reed states as if it's decided, turning the key over and the ignition protests just as much as I do. He keeps telling me that. He's been saying it for weeks trying to get me to change my mind.

"I'm going in there," I say and my voice bellows with more anger than I realized I had.

What's between Kat and I may be different. I'm sure as hell different; colder, meaner even. Hell, I don't know how anyone could love me after what I've done behind bars. A tremor runs through my hand and I form a fist to stop it.

"I dreaded a number of things," I confess to my best friend, clearing my throat as I do and making sure to keep my voice even. "I dreaded seeing my father's grave, I dreaded seeing my uncle Eamon, now the pres, who barely spoke to me while I was away. I dreaded seeing the fucking club—"

"Don't say that—" He tries to interrupt me, his voice thick with sympathy I never fucking asked for.

The leather groans as I turn to look him in the eye. "It's the truth. Some nights I blamed the fucking club. But I never dreaded seeing you or her." *Until now.*

Gripping the handle in my right, and the strap to a duffle bag with essentials in my left, I swing open the old truck door and listen to it creak as I step out. Spending the night with Reed made me certain of one thing: we're still the same.

"Now I need my hellcat back." A nervousness prickles across my skin as the wind creeps up my leather jacket. "Even if she doesn't want me," I murmur beneath my breath as I hear the slam of Reed's door and then his heavy footsteps quickening to catch up to me. "She fucking owes me."

All I could think about every night was walking up these concrete porch steps. As Reed races to beat me to the door, using the iron knocker, I'm all too aware of how I pictured walking right in. Not stopping or hesitating in the least. She'd stand there, her eyes wide first with shock, then relief and adoration.

Sometimes that's what I pictured as I fell asleep on that

hard bed with images of her writhing under me in my head.

Other times, my eyes stayed open as I stared at the cracked ceiling of the cell, imagining how she'd back away, how she'd tell me she couldn't be with a man like me. That she knew what I'd done and that I was all wrong for her. That everything we ever were was a mistake.

She told me then, in these fucking terrors that kept me wide awake just like it did last night, that she regretted ever being with me and it was over.

I prepare myself for whatever it is she has to say as a voice I know all too well calls out, "Coming!"

If she's going to leave me, she's going to have to do it to my face.

"I think this is a mistake." Reed's murmur is spoken just beneath his breath, as is my response.

"I'll add it to my fucking résumé."

The crickets are the only sounds I can hear over my racing heart until the door opens.

Thump, thump. The light of the foyer creates a golden halo around her. Standing all of five feet two, Kat stares up at me, her gorgeous eyes working their way up from my chest until she meets my gaze. Her expression isn't at all how I pictured.

Time pauses for a moment. It's gone too fast, but it stills long enough for me to take in her cherry lips, her hazel eyes and the shock that disappears far too quickly, replaced with a shadow that hides a woman I used to know.

Thump, thump. The door opens with a groan and she stands to the side, her gaze moving easily from me to Reed as she tells us to come in. Her cadence is soft but confident, and I nearly second-guess everything until she peeks up at me and her grip on the door tightens.

There's the look I've been dreaming up, staring back at me through a glossy gaze. It's nearly gone as quickly as I see it, but I know damn well it's there as she glances to the floor and licks her lips. I don't take my eyes from her and she's quick to bring hers back up but it stops at my mouth.

Heat spikes through my blood. *That's my needy girl.*

Even if she doesn't openly admit it, even if she's wary, she wants me still. The tension crackles between us, although it's quickly extinguished.

"I could smell the beer and whiskey from all the way in the kitchen," Lydia states evenly with a touch of humor as she leans against the open doorway through Kat's home.

I've seen pictures of this place, Reed showed me. He kept tabs on her for me. And although the compliment is there—*I like your place*—there's not a word that could leave my dried throat right now even if I tried.

It's silent and awkward between Kat and me as Reed makes small talk with Lydia and I share stolen glances with the woman I never stopped loving.

Her thin cotton nightgown barely hides her curves although it's baggy on her small frame. I know I've aged while

I've been gone, with dark circles under my eyes that never used to be there and lines from constant stress and worry, but Kat's changed too. Without an ounce of makeup on her, there are bags under her eyes and I wonder if it's because she couldn't sleep knowing I'd be knocking on her door tonight. Her hair is shorter, cut just above her shoulders and dyed a pretty blond that complements her olive skin tone.

Kat walks past me, careful not to brush against me, to stand beside Lydia and motions to the stairs at my right. The instinct to slip my arm around her waist and pin her against the wall is only stopped by her statement when she says, "The guest room is ready for you."

Thump, thump. I want nothing more than to hold her but instead I'm paralyzed where I am. A fucking guest room?

A chill flows through me, keeping me where I am and threatening to take her away again if I say or do anything at this moment.

Reed clears his throat and Kat crosses her arms, refusing to look at him. A beat passes and I finally speak.

"You two not friends anymore?" I motion between the two of them, although my gaze traps Kat's and my pulse rages against my veins. She swallows thickly before answering me with a gentleness that tells me she's feeling the same thing I am. That all of this is balanced on a cord wound so tight it may break.

"He didn't tell me you were coming," she says and licks

her lower lip before adding with a sigh, "I had to find out from Lydia."

It's only now that I realize I'm far too drunk for this. *Fuck.*

I stand there, time ticking away, just taking her in. My eyes roam down her body and back up and although I want her more than anything, I can't help but to notice how her bottom lip wobbles and she catches it between her teeth. It's telling me the same thing that her glossy eyes and her defensive posture are.

Two strong hands press against my back. "We had a lot to drink, so," Reed states, pushing me forward but I'm far from ready. Even if the alcohol is wearing on me, making my head spin and throwing off my balance.

The question comes out without my conscious consent. "You don't want me here?"

"I didn't say that—" She raises her voice for the first time, her gaze piercing through mine with thinly veiled desperation.

Reed shoves at my back. "You're drunk, man, come on."

My grip loosens and the duffle bag drops to my feet. "I need to hear you say it," I blurt out and then catch myself. Fuck, she makes me weak. She has me under her thumb and doesn't even know it.

"Say what?" she's quick to ask and that eagerness promises she'll say what I want to hear, but I'm too much of a bitch to risk it.

"Tell me you want me to stay here," I say instead and then

I'm quick to amend it. "That it's all right that I stay with you."

Reed bends at my side, picking up the duffle bag and not looking at either of us.

Lydia looks anywhere but at us too and all the while, I wait.

"Of course you can ... I'm just," she says and glances down, then back up at me, "... I'm just surprised you want to." Her voice nearly breaks and the corners of her lips turn down.

Fuck. I hate this. I hate every moment of it as a cold sweat breaks out on the back of my neck.

It kills me how she looks as if she's on the verge of breaking down. Lydia must see it too because she's quick to tell me to get my drunk ass upstairs. "Welcome home," she adds before stepping between Kat and me.

I can't help myself, though. I ask her, "Did you think I forgot about you? I know you haven't forgotten about me."

"Let's go," Reed says and grabs my arm, pulling me to the stairs as Lydia takes Kat's hand, taking her away from me.

In all the ways I imagined coming back to her, this sure as hell wasn't the reality I expected. That's all I can think as I climb up the stairs, wishing I'd had enough beer to pass out at the fucking bar so I could have avoided all of this.

At one point I was strong for her, but after four years, all I feel is broken or pissed off and there's no in between until I look at her ...

I barely know who I am anymore, but all I want to know is whether or not she could love me again.

CHAPTER 3

KAT

Seeing the two of them together is surreal. Reed ... and most notably Cillian. My heart is all sorts of crushed yet still able to beat. Furiously and nervously at the same time. With my fingers numb and barely able to breathe, I watch, unable to say a word.

Although I grimace as Cill stumbles and my chest flips with an ache. My Cillian. My rock and my ride or die ... he's a shell of the man he used to be.

He's still handsome and every bit of how I remember him ... but four years in prison aged him, obviously so. He doesn't seem to have slept a bit, given that darkness under his eyes. He's more than toned now. The muscles that ripple in his shoulders and down his arms pull at the cotton of his shirt as his leather jacket falls to the floor.

Sexy and sinful ... but there's a brokenness that's undeniable. Even as he attempted to hide it when I opened the door, I felt it. In the very marrow of my bones, my body ached in mourning of what's become of him.

I always knew him to be deadly and brooding even, but this is a different brokenness.

It takes everything in me not to gather him up myself and let out these sobs.

It's been a year since I've seen him and that year must have been hell.

Regret pulls my gaze away as Reed mutters, "Come on. You're drunk," yet again.

Judging by Reed's scowl, he's on the verge of pulling Cill out of my house by the arm and back to his truck. I should let him do it. This whole thing—Cill staying with me after his release, no warning—it shouldn't be happening. No one has the right to show up at my house and demand to stay with me. But I know I'll never forgive myself if I let this happen.

Cill is in no state to go anywhere else. He's drunk, and there's a darkness in his eyes that scares me because I don't think he's able to hold back a single thing. It also begs me to comfort him.

My fingers itch at my side and as they do, Lydia tugs at my arm and silently mouths the word *no* as if she could read my mind.

I hate everything about this moment.

The tension between the four of us is so thick it makes my heart pound. Reed's about to get physical with him. Drag him out of here, back to his truck.

"You shouldn't even be driving," I tell Reed without looking at him, my arms crossed as I sink back into the chair, Lydia standing as if she's my warden by my side.

Reed mutters, "I'm not driving."

"You drove here," I bite back and peek up at him, but he's still focused on Cill.

"I'll walk home. I needed to drop him off. But we'll both leave now." Both leave. My heart stalls in protest and everything goes cold.

"No," Cill states with finality.

Cill's hardly spoken to me but I could easily hear the slight slur in his voice, and I can barely look him in the eye. I have no idea what Reed told him about me. I don't know what Cill knows. Which only intensifies the betrayal that overwhelms me.

Two drunk men, four years of hell for all of us, and a stubborn man who doesn't know what's good for him anymore ... shit.

This is going to turn into a fight. It's an invitation for the cops to get nosy. Cill doesn't need that. I don't need that.

"Let him go and head home," I tell Reed. "You can come back for your truck in the morning."

"You sure about this, because—" He doesn't get a chance to finish as Cill interrupts. "I'll go upstairs," he says, then clears his throat and the cords in his neck tighten as he swallows, "and you walk home. She's right."

Cill shakes off Reed's arm and balances himself on the banister. My God, the pull I feel to him as he closes his eyes and steadies his breath.

Reed tosses Cill's duffle bag toward the foot of the stairs, nodding. Lydia offers him a ride, which he rejects and then he and I share a look. One that brings that ache back tenfold.

"Come on," I say and open the door for Reed. I shoo him away, but I stand on the porch and make sure he doesn't drive. I don't think Reed is as drunk as Cill, but he definitely shouldn't be behind the wheel.

When he's gone, I shut the door and lock it, then push the deadbolt shut and set the code too. I can feel Cill standing behind me. His very presence is throwing heat into the room.

So for a long moment, I keep my back to him, doing everything I can to not tremble and keep my composure.

Lydia shuffling around in the kitchen is the only thing I can hear. I wish the creak of the stairs would tell me Cillian's doing what he said he would, but he's not. When I turn, he's right where he was before but fully turned around, his light blue gaze focused right on me. Those big, wounded puppy dog eyes don't match the brutality of this man in the least.

A cabinet opens and then closes to the left of us.

Lydia's lingering in the kitchen to give us space, I bet, and I'm glad she did. I can't have this moment with Cill in front of anyone else. Not her. Not Reed.

"I think I might be drunk, Hellcat," he rumbles and his lips kick up into an asymmetrical smile I've missed. All of that apprehension vanishes and it's something else that forces me forward, one step at a time.

Hearing that nickname in his voice, drunk and scratchy and tired, makes me go weak in the knees.

My response is gentle and somehow comes out even. "You should probably go to bed, then." Standing a safe three feet away from him, I cross my arms over my chest to keep my hands where they are. His gaze drops, making note of it. A sad smile on his face is all I'm given.

I swallow thickly and head up the stairs to the second floor, past him, my arm brushing against his. And when we touch, my God, that small touch. My eyes close and I breathe in deep, quickening my pace when I hear the stairs creaking behind me with his weight.

A narrow hall leads to a bedroom in the back. Cill appears beside me with his duffle bag slung over one shoulder. He looks at the room. The bed. The window. It's not much, but enough for a guest to be comfortable.

"You want me to go somewhere else?" he asks again.

"No," I say and my answer is firm even if it is just a whisper between us. I don't need any time to think about it.

It surprises me how much I mean it. I don't want him to go anywhere else.

"Stay here," I tell him and back up when he takes a half step forward. "You're drunk tonight," I explain as his arm drops to his side. "Tomorrow." I say the word like it's a promise.

With a nod and a hint of that asymmetric smile, he repeats, "Tomorrow."

"Good night, Cill."

"Good night, Hellcat."

I almost give in. I almost recklessly go to him. Even with every logical thought that's guarding my heart, part of me wants to feel his lips on mine again more than the rest of me wants to confess my sins and tell him what happened.

But in the end, I pull the door closed.

The act pulls on strings I'd rather stay still. I only hold it together then and there to tell Lydia she can go home if she wants. She only hesitates a moment.

My hands tingle with anticipation as I climb the stairs, my heart thumping with every step.

Before going to my room, I check on Cill's but the door is closed and I don't have it in me to open it.

My own bed feels empty in a way it never has before.

My body craves to be wrapped around Cill, but my fingers tangle in my hair instead. There's so much to tell him and each line runs wild in my mind. There's so much I already should have told him.

Sleep evades me. The thought of him down the hall, alone under the covers, is too much. It keeps me awake.

I toss and turn, the sheets uncomfortably tight and all wrong. Every time I glance at the clock, it's only been ten minutes and yet hours tick by. And then another. All the while I stare at my bedroom door.

Should I go to him? I don't even know if Cill would want that. Even if he did right now, he may not after we talk.

Time changes everything.

Tears form at the corners of my eyes and I brush them away, struggling to hold on to my sanity. It's difficult not to dwell on the negatives, the thoughts that keep me wide awake. Instead, I think about what used to be. How at one point, I thought all we had left was our happily ever after.

With the memories playing back like a movie, sleep comes and goes in short spurts.

Dreams tempt me and they show me how it once was when we first got together.

Morning comes all too soon with a stubborn alarm and tired, reddened eyes.

"Fuck," I mutter as I smack the clock, hating that I didn't turn it off last night. Six a.m. is far too early and puts me at only three hours of restless sleep at most.

Still, I don't bother to stay under the sheets.

As soon as I remember—Cill's here—I'm out of the bed, my bare feet on the cold wooden floor. It's not far to his room, but when I get there the door is wide open. I know what that means before I step through the threshold.

My palms are clammy as I steady my breathing.

He's not there.

With a quick check in the bathroom only to find nothing, I head downstairs. I rush down, taking the stairs two at a time. The house is quiet around me. When I don't see him, I call out his name and it echoes in the empty house.

He's not here either. I circle the living room to look for signs of him. There are none. He didn't sit on the couch, or pull the throw blanket over his legs.

Swallowing thickly, I do everything I can to shake off the uncertainty.

I don't know why I care so much. He spent one night in my house, and it's not like there would be plenty of evidence that he was here. As the heat of panic creeps up my arms, I just need some proof. Some little thing to say Cill's really back home and last night wasn't a dream. He was here with me.

As I head to the living room to grab my phone that's charging, ready to text Lydia, I see the note.

A slim piece of paper from the notepad I use to make grocery lists. He didn't leave me with nothing after all.

It's from Cill.

I have to take care of a few things.

Like getting a phone ...

I'll call you and I'll see you tonight.

If you need anything, or you need me, call Reed.

SIX YEARS AGO

A younger version of Cill, only seventeen years old, leaned over the pool table. Shot after shot, he cleared the table with ease. He was a shark even then. I remember thinking he probably learned how to play from his dad, but I didn't care about that. All I cared about was how hot he looked in the dim lights of the rec room. He wore a tight black T-shirt that showed off his muscular arms. Sinking a ball into one of the pockets, easy as can be, he looked up at me. A smirk immediately met his lips. He didn't disguise how much he wanted me and I didn't attempt to hide anything either. He let his eyes linger on my face for a long time, until I blushed.

Our fathers were doing business upstairs. They did that a lot and left the two of us alone. I met Cill's father before I met Cill. He told me more than once he thought Cill and I would get along well. Which is probably why my father never brought me to the MC club ... until that night.

"You want to play?" Cill asked.

"I don't know how."

"Bullshit." He grinned at me and every inch of me went hot. "You're Angelo's daughter. You trying to hustle me?" My teeth caught my lower lip, although it didn't help hide my smile. "Little con artist, aren't you?"

"Maybe." I picked at the torn jeans I wore.

"What were you going to bet me, then?" I blushed deeper, imagining all the things I could say if I had the courage. "'Cause I was going to bet you a kiss."

"If you won, you wanted a kiss from me?" I questioned him. The idea of Cill wanting a kiss from me was like winning the lottery. Even if it never happened, that didn't matter. He wanted a kiss from me, and I could barely breathe with how excited that made me.

I knew he could tell. I wasn't very good at hiding anything. His growing smile forced away any insecurity I had.

Unfortunately, it didn't last for long.

Both our fathers clattered down the stairs at that moment, their voices coming into the rec room ahead of them. I didn't get to hear Cill's answer, if he gave me one. I fell in love with him in that moment. I never stood a chance. He was sexy and sinful ... but charming and easy in a way I'd never felt before. There was an attraction I couldn't deny on my side and he wanted me back. Nothing was ever going to top that.

Nothing.

CHAPTER 4

CILLIAN

Four years might as well have been a fucking lifetime.

Slipping the new phone into my back pocket, I attempt to take in everything that's changed and what has stayed the same.

Life used to be routine and easy. I loved every fucking day.

Monday through Saturday I worked my shift in the garage, fixing up whatever came in. Unless we had a run, in which case it was days on end with the growl of the bike under me. Either way, work came and went easy enough and with good company.

Church, a.k.a. the club meetings, on Sunday and then family dinner after.

My father told me when I got out, he'd make sure everything was like it was before.

Now he's six feet under and I would give anything to hear him offering me any advice at all to get through this.

The slow rumble of the truck keeps us company as I keep my ass in the seat, not knowing what to expect next.

"You look like today kicked your ass," Reed comments half-heartedly as I turn off the engine and close the door to his truck.

"Thanks." I huff a laugh and think back on Kat's house. It's small and in need of a powerwash and weeding. The whole house could use fixing up here and there.

I could do that. I could so easily take care of it for her.

"Rough night?"

I shrug before dragging my focus back to him. His hands are already covered in oil, just as mine will be in a few hours. My uncle didn't waste any time putting me back to work. One other thing has stayed the same as well. Church is on Sunday and I'm damn well looking forward to that. Until then, he told me to stick with Reed in the garage.

"It was all right. Slept off the beer and snuck out before she got up," I tell him.

"Snuck out?" He lets out a chuckle, a smile growing on his face. "I know I keep saying it," he starts, "but I missed you, man. We all missed you."

At that remark, my thoughts run back to Kat. Reed must know it because he tells me, "She missed you. Trust me, man, she missed you."

I stopped by her bedroom door at the crack of fucking dawn this morning and thought about pushing it open, but I didn't.

Reed left his keys to the truck on the kitchen table. I drove it to get a few things I needed, texted Reed I'd meet him here at the garage and waited and waited. He only lives a few houses down and I thought about heading to his place instead; I couldn't fucking stand to stay inside the garage. Being there when it's empty and ghosts linger in every room, was more than I could take. So I stayed in the truck, waiting for his ass to get here.

I've never felt so fucking out of place in my life.

As our boots crunch on the gravel, he passes me one of the two cups of coffee from the corner shop. It's cheap, like it's always been, but hot. "You and Kat talk last night?"

"No."

"You sleep all right?"

Nodding, I comment, "Pretty good," which doesn't do it justice.

For the first time in years, there were no lights shining in my eyes in the middle of the night. No fights. No screaming. Nobody losing his shit from being behind bars. It was the best sleep I've had since I went away. Only way it could have been better is if Kat was in the bed with me.

We go up to the third floor, past the garage on the first, then the rec room on the second where my life ended four years ago.

The office is different. It's still shabby in the same way, with secondhand office furniture and filing cabinets, but it's not quite like I recall. Reed takes a seat in an old office chair behind one of the desks and I take the leather sofa across from him that I don't remember from before. At least one thing has been updated.

The garage doesn't open for another thirty minutes, so we've got time to kill.

"What's it like with my uncle being in charge now?" I remember back in the day when he and my dad would go at it.

Reed's thumb taps on the armrest, a telltale sign that's always given away when he's anxious.

"If I'm honest, I miss your pops."

He died while I was in prison. I didn't get to attend his funeral, and it's one of my bigger regrets. I should have been there for that. Instead, I was in a cramped cell reading a warden-approved paperback book about metalworking.

"And things are still unsettled?"

"It's more about the leadership now." Reed rubs a hand over his face. "Duncan Tray, that prick from up north, tried to step in and negotiate with our contracts … so when your uncle insisted on voting for change, we went with it at first."

"At first?" I hate that fucker Duncan with everything in me. When I was locked away, I know he paid people on the inside to fuck with me. He's lucky he's still breathing.

"Some of the members want to move into a bigger space and expand the operation. And others want to stay where we are, with what we have."

"What do you think?"

Reed searches my eyes for a moment before telling me he's one of the few who doesn't feel comfortable expanding. "Your uncle wants to, though, and he hasn't dropped it. It's just ... we're heading past the territories we have agreements with."

He's tense, barely moving other than the nervous tap of his thumb. "The pres won't let it go."

I can only nod, taking it in and unsure of what this Sunday will be like.

Church was never contentious that I remember. I was young, practically a kid, and I figured things would stay the same forever. Church was for brainstorming ideas for the garage, for fucking around and giving each other a hard time. For splitting cash after handing off deals for the organizations that relied on us. The Cross brothers up north, and the Valettis down south with their connections to the docks. We acted as a go-between and took a hefty chunk of change to make it worthwhile.

"I don't see why we need to expand unless things have changed? Have we lost deals or taken smaller cuts or what?"

"No," he says and his voice raises slightly as he shakes his head, "money is good. There's no reason, that's what I'm saying." He hesitates and pauses his tapping before saying, "It should have been you who took over."

All I can do is swallow down his statement with both bitterness and loss. I always knew eventually I'd take over my dad's place in the MC. Years and years and years from now when my pops was gray haired and didn't want to do it anymore.

Life's a bitch.

For the second time today, I miss my father. If I closed my eyes right now, I could see him sitting there in place of my best friend. He sat in that seat nearly all my life.

My throat is so tight, I can't even offer an opinion. I haven't been back long enough to know which path is the right way forward. I haven't been out long enough to know what I want to do with myself, let alone make a decision that would affect the club.

"You'll vote with me on Sunday?" Reed questions nervously and I don't hesitate to nod in agreement.

"Yeah," I answer, my tone reflecting my apprehension given everything that's changed.

"Sorry, man ... it's mostly good." Reed shakes off the tension and relaxes his shoulders as he changes the subject. "You looking forward to seeing everyone?"

The coffee hasn't cured my hangover yet and I don't want to answer questions about prison. Many of the guys in the MC have been in jail for one thing or another, but I'm the most recent, the youngest ... and I took the fall when any of them could have done it instead.

The more I think about it, the angrier I get.

"Yeah." I clear my throat and tell him, "It's good to be home, I just … need a moment to get reacquainted I guess."

I took the fall for the raid, and they've been careful since then. It makes me bitter to think about it. If Kat's dad hadn't fucked around the way he did four years ago, I wouldn't have lost her, I wouldn't have gone away and I would have been here when my pops's health started going south.

Leaning back, I settle on something that brings a smile to both of us. "I'm looking forward to working on my bike," I say.

"Working on her?" He grins and tells me, "I fixed her up so she's practically brand new."

I chuckle, nodding my gratitude.

My mind wanders to Kat. Thinking she's all sorts of new to me too.

New and apparently off-limits. Or so she thinks.

Even if I can't touch her, I want to be in that house. Wanting that soft bed with her scent on it. In prison I had to sit with all these feelings. There was literally nothing else to do. I could try to jog them out in the exercise yard, but I was in my cell most of the day. You learn to deal with the waves of rage. Some guys do, anyway. Other guys go crazy in there. Who knows? Maybe I was one of them.

Reed eventually does some work on the computer. He makes a few calls. My uncle comes in and the three of us have

SEXY AS SIN   57

a conversation that feels like it goes on forever, but only lasts about fifteen minutes. I'm getting back to life in the club. This is life in the club.

The garage is where I lose most of my time, remembering what could have been.

Working with metal and surrounded by the nostalgic smell of oil, the feel of labor bringing a burn to my muscles forces the time to tick by. For the first time since I've been out, there's a moment of peace and ease. And naturally ... my mind wanders back to her.

It always comes back to her.

It's not until I climb into Reed's truck, and he gets in behind the wheel that he brings her up. "You two ...? What's going on there?"

"I haven't spoken to her in a year," I tell him. He's busy nodding his head while I admit, "But I want her back. I want us back."

I keep my last thought unspoken as he turns over the engine: *I need her back.* If I have her, everything else will be right again. I fucking know it will.

I'll make it right. I'll make her love me again.

Chapter 5

Kat

Lydia leans against my kitchen counter and looks out the window into the yard. Her takeout container is open on the countertop next to her and she pokes her fork into it, then scoops out another minuscule bite. "I'm going to miss this."

"This restaurant is only good about half the time," I joke, downplaying her somber mood.

"I'm going to miss you, Kat."

She rolls her eyes at me and laughs, but I know the emotion behind her words is real. Realer than most things in my life, anyway. Some things turned out to be cruel jokes and I didn't know until after the fact. C'est la vie, I suppose.

"I'm happy for you. I truly am." I snag a wonton and add, "But I'm going to miss you like crazy." I can't even look her in the eye as I say it. Just in case some part of me decides to get weepy.

I know how much she's wanted to go to college and how excited she is to start her new life. Part of me actually considered leaving to stay with her, at her suggestion a few months back when she got her acceptance letter in the spring. But ... I don't think my life is anything to dismiss, either. My job at the flower shop is a good one, I love it even. I have a kind boss and reasonable hours and I enjoy putting the orders together. It's meaningful, what I do, even if it is small. It's just not college. Lydia going off to college feels like another world away.

In reality, it's only a two-hour ride on the train. I know which ticket to buy to visit her and how long it'll take to get there. I even know some of the places we can check out when I visit. We mapped it all out over a bottle of wine when we checked out the campus together. In all honesty, I've never been so thrilled for her. Lydia's eyes were so bright when she took in the buildings.

With my fork halfway in the air, I cock a brow and ask with a smirk, "You sure you have to leave me all alone down here?"

She's drinking wine with her takeout—we both are. I'm not drunk, but I feel the effects of the alcohol. Maybe that's why I'm only thinking of Cill every five minutes. I'm aware it's every five minutes because I can't stop checking the clock. He texted me when he'd be home.

He said *your place*, rather than home.

I'll be at your place around seven.

It's six forty-five now.

With the cabernet sinking in sip by sip, I'm less nervous and more excited than I've been all day. Warm. A little bit calmer. Lydia takes another swallow of hers.

"I'm not leaving you alone." She glances toward the stairs. "Am I?"

I can't think of what to say to Lydia, so I grab the wine instead. I'm anxious with the thought of him in the house. Anxious, and attracted. Another sip down and I shrug, licking the sweet liquid from my lower lip.

All my feelings for him came back in a rush with that simple text message. Thinking of him in that guest bedroom made it damn hard to settle down at night. I'm not the kind of girl who tosses and turns over things she can't control, but Cill? He's like a thunderstorm. I never know when he might break apart.

My gaze flicks to the clock again as I lean forward in anticipation. Shoving the food away, I can't eat anymore with these butterflies.

He wants me. I don't know everything and I have to tell him what happened. But the man I've always loved wants me and there's still something there.

My only worry is that once I tell him what happened, or once he finds out, he'll never look at me the same. But last night, that look he gave me …

"How did it go last night?" Lydia asks, bringing my attention back to her although she's focused elsewhere. She's watching out the window again.

"Not a peep from him after I showed him the room, and when I got up … he was gone." I rub under my still sore eyes. I'm exhausted, but there's not a chance in hell I'm going to bed until I see him.

"You sleep at all?"

"Not at all." I can barely manage a fake smile. I don't count those hours when I was half dreaming close to the morning. That wasn't restful sleep.

"Kat," she says, her tone scolding. "You have to rest. You can't start losing sleep over—"

"I'll be all right. Just getting used to things. It was the first night." And I didn't know it was coming. All things considered, things could have gone a lot worse. Cill's back home and he's safe. I was safe in my house. No one tried to break in. If losing a night of sleep is the worst that happens, I'll be counting my blessings.

"You know," Lydia says, "you are the one in control here. If you don't want him here, you tell him that. He can find somewhere else to go."

"I know."

I understand the worry that lingers in her eyes. I do. I get it. But it's Cill. And if there's something there still, how could

I possibly let that go?

I took it upon myself to be independent so that I'd never be caught off guard the way I was that night at the clubhouse. No one would ever throw my life into disarray again. But I know, right away, that I won't kick Cill out of my house and I won't say no if he wants me. I don't think I have that in me. Even if he is turning my emotions a bit upside down.

A bit—okay. Totally upside down.

"And ..." She takes another small bite of her food. "If you don't want to be with him, you don't have to be."

"I know."

"Then why do you look like that?"

"Like what?"

"Like you're stuck and hopeless. And maybe like you're a lovesick lost puppy." Lydia softens her statement with a smile.

She's right. I couldn't even nap today. I spent an hour on the couch trying, but all I could think about was whether Cill would come back or whether he'd disappear out of my life again. I thought about his note. I thought about him ... and then he texted me.

"It's kind of insulting to my ego that a single text from a man can make me feel this way," I admit out loud and, without my conscious consent, sneak a peek at the clock again.

Lydia snorts a laugh and pushes her hair out of her face, elbows on the table while dragging out the words, "Oh my God. You still love him!"

There's that twist in my chest and the knowledge I have to tell him everything, but still I nod.

"So you're a mess over him, even after four years?"

"Because I want him with me more than anything," I admit. "But when he finds out what happened ..." Emotion makes my throat close.

"So you haven't told him?" Lydia questions.

"I betrayed him, Lydia." The clock reads six fifty-five. "I honestly thought about texting him ... and then hiding at your place." A heavy exhale leaves me.

"He wasn't here," she tells me and I'm shocked by the hard tone she uses. With my gaze trapped in hers mostly from shock, she repeats, "He wasn't here and a lot happened. He changed and so did you, and if he can't understand that, it's on him." Her swallow is audible when she finishes and she gives me a curt nod as if to ask, isn't that right?

There's a flop in my chest, one that's dull and thuds on its own for a moment.

"How do I look him in the eye after he's gone through hell and tell him what happened?" I've thought of it a million times, but even in my imagination, I open my mouth and no words come out.

"Kat." Her voice goes soft and serious. Lydia puts down her fork and my stomach twists at the conversation I know is coming. "You aren't the only one, and he needs to know—"

The front door rattles, then opens with a familiar creak.

I jump, feeling guilty and caught, and barely manage to catch my wine before it sloshes all over my kitchen floor.

"We're back," Reed says. "You here?"

"In the kitchen," Lydia calls out. With only a few steps Reed appears in the threshold, wearing his leathers, complete with a Celtic cross, and an easy smile. Until he sees me, and it slips for a moment.

Then there's Cill ... appearing right behind him and all that nervousness and fluttering and every emotion that I can't control, it all comes up full force with no way to stop it.

CHAPTER 6

CILLIAN

With a soft click, the front door shuts behind me and my gaze roams down Kat's backside as she enters a code into the security system.

My body's hot and my blood pounds as I slip off my leather jacket and wait for her to turn around.

To face me and face this situation we're in.

It's so quiet in her place that I can easily hear her swallow as my jacket is placed over the back of the simple wooden chair.

"Well, now they're gone ..." she says and trails off as she ambles her way into the kitchen, her bare feet padding on the floor. With her arms crossed over her chest, she hides the fact that she's not wearing a bra under her dark navy sleep shirt.

"Do you need anything before I go to bed?" she asks,

brushing her hair off her shoulder, her wide hazel eyes peering up at me.

"Why does what you say to me, not match what I think … you're thinking. What is it you really want to say?" I take a hesitant step toward her and the floor creaks beneath me.

My little hellcat stays where she is, her breath hitching as I reach out and let my thumb slip down her arm. The small touch is like a spark, cracking and igniting the faint tinder into a blazing fire.

She swallows again, her chest heaving with a desperate inhale before brushing my touch away and ripping her gaze from me as well.

I haven't felt so nervous, so close to the edge of something that could break me since I sat in that small barren room of the courthouse, signing confession papers and knowing it meant I wouldn't see freedom again for years.

That's what her simple act of rejection does to me … it's worse than that even. Fuck.

"I um …" She clears her throat, her back to me as she gathers the wine and glasses, cleaning up the small space and avoiding me entirely.

With both hands gripping the back of the chair, I'm careful as I ask her, "Do you want to talk? Do you want me to help?" It takes everything in me to keep my voice steady as I confess to her, "I'll even take small talk, Hellcat."

I'm only given her profile as she rinses out the glasses, the sound of the water rushing from the faucet taking up space, but her laugh, feminine and warm, drowns it out. She still loves to be called Hellcat. Hope lingers and the heat rises.

I may be nervous, but I'm not letting her push me away.

"Small talk, like what?" She peeks up at me, turning off the faucet.

"Thought you preferred beer."

She huffs a short laugh, wine staining her bottom lip. "Things changed ..." In an instant, that warmth vanishes. She's hot and cold. "I have to tell you—"

"No you don't." My response is harder than I thought it would be.

"I don't want to talk about ... whatever the hell it is that keeps stealing you from me."

"I can't—" Her head shakes and her reluctance shows as she grips the counter, no longer facing me in the least when she adds, "I can't stand seeing you without telling you—"

Reed did this same shit on and off before I got out. Everyone wants to fill me in on the bad shit.

"Stop," I say, cutting her off. Everyone I love is holding back and, for the love of God, I just need them there. "I just got out," I tell her. Emotions riddle the words and because of that, and maybe because I take a step toward her, she faces me again. Vulnerable but wanting. I soften my tone, offering her the parts of me she loves. "Can't I just have a moment where I see you smile again?"

I used to tell her that her smile made it all okay. No matter what shit we were in, no matter how fucked anything got, if she was smiling it would all be all right and just like back then, she offers me one. Her gaze falls to the floor as the shy smile I've held on to for years to carry me through this hell settles on her lips.

With one more step, I close the gap between us to tell her, "That's my girl." This time I cup her cheek, my thumb falling on those lips I used to devour.

Both of her hands wrap around my wrist and I think she's going to pull my hand away, but she doesn't.

Longing is etched into the shards of green and gold in her gaze. Then in a blink, it's over. "I'm really tired," she tells me and it's my cue to drop my hand.

"Didn't sleep last night?"

"Yeah ..." she answers and peeks up at me again, the tension still there but held back so carefully. "... just wanted to stay up in case you needed something."

"I'm good," I tell her softly and add, "You should go to bed."

There's a moment I think she'll kiss me. That she'll pop up on her tiptoes like she used to and give me even the smallest of pecks. My chest thumps and my blood rushes, knowing if she does, I'll fucking devour her.

I'll take her right here and now.

Instead, the moment passes and I watch her go. I wait for her to look back, and she does, at the very top of the stairs. She grips the banister and her lips part like she'll say something, but then she stops herself and all I'm given is another *sleep well*.

I could. Ten seconds before she's gone and that's when I can breathe. With both hands on the table, I lean over forcing myself to stay right the fuck where I am.

I'll give her a moment. I'll let her climb into bed and then I'm going up there.

Rounding the table, I tour her place, picking up odds and ends here and there. Getting a good look at who she is now. Little bits of her show in accent pillows with deep jewel tones and soft blankets laid out on the back of the sofa.

It's not until I open the drawer in the coffee table that my composure crumbles. There's not only a framed photo of the two of us tucked away, but also my leather patch I gave her. The one my mother used to wear that I gave Kat the day after I told her I loved her for the first time.

It's right there, in the heart of her home, but hidden away so no one can see.

Slamming the drawer shut, I run my hand through my hair and second-guess my plan, but only for a moment. Taking the stairs two at a time, I head upstairs and any hesitation I had vanishes when I see her bedroom door open.

It wasn't this morning. It was firmly shut.

It's pitch black inside and as I push the door open, it creaks. It takes a moment for my eyes to adjust.

And a moment for her to see I'm there.

"Cillian?" she asks in a hushed voice, breathless even.

"Is your bed big enough for the both of us?" I question, my hand already on the door to close it.

With the light filtering in from the stairwell and the lights left on downstairs, they offer a halo around Kat and I'm able to see her nod a yes.

Thank fuck, I nearly groan in satisfaction as I close the door.

My boots come off first, followed by my jeans and then my shirt. My back was to her for the first part, but as I tug off my shirt, I catch sight of her watching.

If we were as we used to be, I'd tease her. I'd ask her if she liked what she saw.

In my mind I see her, I see us: a different version that was never broken and she'd bite her lower lip, sitting up and teasing me back to come see for myself.

A pang in my chest of regret and guilt stays with me as the comforter rustles and the bed groans as I climb in.

She's silent and perfectly still on her side of the bed. Waiting, and more than likely overthinking things.

As casually as I can, I roll onto my side and tell her, "I want to hold you."

It's dark and the shadows play on her gorgeous face but I can perfectly see her defenseless gaze. Carefully, I lay my arm on hers and my brow cocks as I add, "Please?"

A moment passes and then another before she rolls over

to the other side, scooting closer to me so I can wrap an arm around her.

There's space between us but as the minutes pass, both of us lying there, our warm bodies slowly shift closer together until she settles her ass against my crotch.

I take my time as I slip my thumb down the crook of her neck. Every action is measured. Even when I nuzzle right there and kiss below the shell of her ear.

Her hushed gasp is fucking everything I need to continue. My thumb finds the swell of her breast and she presses her chest into my touch.

It may have been years but I remember that soft gasp where a touch of surprise lingers. The way her eyes nearly close, heavy with lust, is a detail that hardens me even more, although I didn't think it was possible.

As I press my splayed hand against her lower belly and then lower, her back arches, bringing her ass to press against me. Only the thin fabric we both wear under the covers separates us now.

A deep groan leaves me, one of primal need that I can't control.

Kat peeks over her shoulder, looking up at me with a concoction of emotion swirling in her gorgeous hazel eyes. She swallows audibly, not breaking the gaze to tell me, "I used to dream of that sound." The moment she's spoken, it's almost like she wishes she hadn't. As if she'd reach up and grab the words, hide them and never admit that again if she could.

There's a wretched pain that burrows into my chest as she attempts to look away, but I crash my lips against hers, taking the kiss I snuck in here to claim.

Maybe I shouldn't be here. Maybe we shouldn't be doing this. But as she turns in my arms, her hands gripping my shoulders, her legs wrapping around my hips as she clings to me, greedy for more, I don't give a fuck.

She has always been mine. Even though she broke my heart. Even after years of being apart.

She's mine. She'll always be mine.

With my lips at the shell of her ear, I whisper, "Get undressed for me." I'm already aching hard for her, but her eagerness is everything I need.

I swear if she gripped me, if she wrapped her fingers around me in this moment, I'd come undone in an instant.

It's been so damn long and I need her. Fuck, how I need her.

When she's fully undressed, but still hiding from me under the covers, I pull them down and turn her over how I want her.

"I'm going to move the pillow here," I tell her before settling it under her hips so her ass is higher, so her pussy is right there for the taking.

I groan in approval as my hand cups her ass and then finds that sweet entrance between her legs.

"Already wet for me," I murmur and then lean forward, grabbing the back of her neck. "If I didn't come in here to take care of you, were you going to do it yourself?"

As her lips part to answer, I rub circles around her clit and my little hellcat jumps beneath me, writhing from the touch.

Giving her ass a quick smack that makes her jump again, I scold her. "Answer me like the good girl I know you are for me."

"No, I wouldn't have," she groans and when my hand returns to her swollen nub, she moans the sweetest sounds into the pillow.

I only pull away to remove my boxers, taking my time so I'm sure she's aware.

As I get into position, I place my hand on her shoulder, keeping her where I want her.

I whisper, just to be certain, "You want me?"

Her whispered answer is immediate. "Yes."

With my head at her slit, I command her, "Tell me how much."

Turning her upper body as much as she can, her eyes find mine and pierce through me as she whispers, "Please. I need you."

Her chin tilts for a kiss, longing evident in her eyes and the moment my lips meet hers in a gentle kiss, it turns bruising and I thrust into her all the way to the hilt with a single stroke.

Her cries of strangled pleasure fuel me to fuck her faster and harder. To take her and ruin her. I wanted to take it slow and love her for our first time together since all this shit happened.

But the moment I'm inside of her, I can't stop mercilessly taking her with every thrust, each one nearly violent. It's been too fucking long without her. I need to feel her come on my dick more than I need to breathe.

CHAPTER 7

KAT

"I don't want you to think about any of this shit or worry. I just want you to love me," he whispered as I lay limp in bed. "Do you understand?"

As he asked the question, he cleaned between my legs with a wet towel and the sudden touch made me jump, but I was sure to tell him yes. The word spilled from my lips as easily as my pleasure came, one orgasm after the other after the other, bringing me closer and closer to sleep.

It was his kiss, though, soft and gentle on my shoulder and my cheek, then on my lips after he whispered, "Good girl," that lured me into the depths of my dreams.

If he hadn't kissed my shoulder so sweetly as he tucked me in, I'd have thought he secretly hated me. For a moment I truly thought that he hated me. That he knew and he hated me. He fucked me so roughly, so ruthlessly ... leaving me so deliciously used. But the way he held me, melted every insecurity away.

If it weren't for the ache between my thighs, I would keep questioning, *Did last night really happen?*

That's all I can think when I wake up.

Slowly, because of the wine I had last night with Lydia.

Memories filter into the last moments of sleep. Cill next to me in the bed. His mouth on mine. His hands on my body like he had never missed a day of touching me in his life.

Did we really?

I turn over on my back and stretch, feeling the soreness in all my muscles ... and elsewhere. His muscles were hard next to the soft touch of the blankets. It was like waking up after a long, deep sleep, so deep you hardly know you're dreaming until it's over. Everything about it felt right. And ... dangerous.

Dangerous in a way I didn't expect. I don't think Cill would hurt me. Not physically. Never that. Even in his anger, he'd never lay a hand on me. Emotionally, though ... My heart races, thinking back to last night. I'm still in disbelief that he wanted this from me. That he still wants me at all, after four years and the very last year.

Footsteps from the kitchen catch my attention, breaking

up my wandering thoughts. I climb out of the bed faster than I ever have. It doesn't take me long to fetch a clean pair of pajamas and I'm still pulling the shirt down as I head downstairs. My heart never stops this weird racing in my chest. Like if I'm not fast enough, it never happened. If I don't see him now, before he leaves, it all goes away.

I find him in the kitchen, standing at the counter staring out of the window by the sink. In worn jeans and a black cotton T-shirt, with bare feet and stubble lining his jaw he appears laid back, yet still has this intensity and pull about him. It's overwhelming and keeps me from going to him. Instead I stand in the threshold of the kitchen.

Cill turns his head at the sound of my feet padding on the floor. "Morning," he says, letting his eyes drift down my body.

"Hi," I offer shyly and then blush as he gives me a charming, yet cocky smirk. "You look far more rested," he comments and then he turns back to the coffee machine. It drips slowly into the pot.

"I had a little help." I clear my throat and add, "A sleep aid I highly recommend." I can't help my smile as I go to the fridge.

I can feel his eyes on me as I get out a pan and the eggs and start the process of cooking them on the stove. A new pack of English muffins waits by the toaster. Scrambled eggs today. My hands aren't steady enough to get the yolks right any other way. Especially with him watching my every move.

Nervousness and insecurity worm their way into my mind again.

I steal a peek at him over my shoulder and find Cill watching me. He's not smiling and my own vanishes.

"You okay?" I ask him.

He blinks. I wonder if anyone else is asking him whether he's okay. Checking in with him, the way people should after an experience like he's had.

"Yeah," he answers, seeming to shake off the seriousness that overcame him. "I'm good." It doesn't leave me, though. Last night was a moment for us.

Was it only a moment? My pulse seems to skip and a numbness creeps up the back of my neck as I put English muffins in the toaster. I take another covert glance at Cill and watch him run his hand over the back of his neck, like he feels the same. A pricking knowing that even if last night was heaven, we're still living in a hell we didn't choose and can't control.

"Do you want to talk about it?"

Another glance at him. The coffee is almost done brewing. "Do I want to talk about what?"

"What happened in there ... and while you were away." It's better to ask him the question even if he refuses to answer me. I want him to know I can handle the topic.

His sharp blue eyes don't leave mine when he says, "I want

to talk about why you stopped coming."

It's so blunt that it feels like a punch. A chill sweeps down my body as the events tip over like dominoes in my mind. Once the first one fell, they couldn't be stopped. I swallow thickly and try to focus on the pan in front of me. My motions mechanical, I pull the plate closer and tip the eggs onto it. Then the other for Cill.

I don't want to tell him. I don't want him to know anything about what happened.

"So we both have some things we want to keep to ourselves?" he questions.

"You scare me, Cillian."

I look back at him and find him staring, his eyes wide. "Why's that?"

The English muffins pop up and I toss them onto the plates, burning the tips of my fingers in the process. Hissing *fuck* under my breath, I'm quick to stick the tips of my fingers into my mouth.

"You all right?" he asks, the concern real in his voice.

"Yeah," I answer him and gather the courage to answer his question.

All the while, I butter the bread automatically so it melts into the little crevices. As if this isn't a conversation I've been dreading. "You're—you're intense. On edge. Your shoulders are rounded in like you think someone's about to hit you. You look like you might get into a fight."

I part my lips to tell him I saw it happen. I watched him change into this man every time I visited him. Then his father … then everything that happened after.

He's the one who changed first, though. "I just … I'm not used to it being like this." I answer him honestly and my voice cracks at the end. I hate it.

I'm reckless as I toss the butter knife into the sink, and I immediately wish I hadn't. I'm calmer as I put the butter back into the fridge.

His gaze burns into the back of me and I pretend the tension isn't heightened.

"You know I'll never—"

"You'd never put a hand on me," I say, cutting him off, turning to gaze at him so he knows I mean it. "But that doesn't mean … it doesn't mean things aren't different and that we aren't different people now."

"And that we both have secrets," he notes as I reach for the plates.

Swallowing thickly, I answer him, "Yeah, we both have secrets," and place both plates on the table, taking my seat. He stands for a moment, watching and with a fork in hand I look up at him, then motion to the plate.

"I'll tell you something if you tell me something," Cill says, taking the seat across from me and picking up the fork but not eating just yet.

Cill clears his throat and he doesn't look at me while he

speaks. Instead he stares at his plate. "The first time they tried to kill me was in the cafeteria."

"What?" The stunned word leaves me as my fork falls and my body goes numb.

"Competitors ... That fuck Tray, I'm pretty sure." He swallows thickly, then finally looks back at me and says, "Reed made a few calls and found some people, so it didn't happen a lot, but in the beginning ... I thought they were going to kill me, Kat." His voice is hoarse with raw emotion although his eyes don't reflect it. His body is tight until he turns his attention back to the plate.

Tears prick the back of my eyes. There's something about how he sits there, so matter of fact that they tried to kill him and that's why he changed. He had to fight for his life. The boy I loved had a tenderness about him that's all but hardened into unforgivable stone. I watched it happen and I couldn't stop it. I couldn't help him ... I didn't even know what he was dealing with. Before I have a chance to calm down and blink the tears back, they leak from the corner of my eyes.

Fuck. It comes out of nowhere.

It's all the pent-up feelings of the last four years coming out of me in a rush. I'm out of my seat, hiding my face from Cill before he can see. I reach for a mug and pretend like I'm not losing it from his confession, but a sob is torn from me. He thought he was going to die. That they were going to kill him and he never told me or anyone. He lived with that fear.

I could never imagine—

Strong arms wrap around me and Cill turns me in his arms, holding me tighter as I try to bury my face in his shirt. It only makes me cry harder. It's been so long since anyone held me like this. He rocks me as he holds me, kissing my hair. "Don't worry, Hellcat. Don't worry. Everything's all right now."

"I'm so sorry." Embarrassment heats my cheeks. "I can't control it ... I just." My throat is tight and the right words won't come. "Neither of you told me." I barely get out the words as Cill loosens his grip slightly to look down at me.

"Why would I, Kat? You couldn't do anything to help me. No one could."

My hands tremble as I furiously wipe away the tears and try to stop. "I'm sorry."

"You didn't do this." He kisses my cheek. "And I don't want to hear you say that to me ever fucking again."

I nod. His grip on me is strong. Stronger than it ever was when we were younger. His years in prison hardened him, aged him. They made his body different than I remember, yet it still feels familiar enough that I crave it.

His hand stays on my back, rubbing soothing circles as I sniffle and make a cup of coffee like I didn't just have a fucking breakdown at the very beginning of our conversation.

Even as I scoop sugar out for the cup, my hand trembles. I just can't imagine, day in and day out, trying not to die.

"Now you tell me something," he murmurs into my ear. Cill doesn't release me as easily as I thought he would. He squeezes me tighter for a second before he lets me go. It hurts to push away from him. I steady myself with a hand on his shoulder and he lets me.

"I—" It's so difficult to speak, even more difficult to focus on one thing. But through my racing thoughts, one truth begs to be spoken. Something that might make him happy. "I stopped coming ... but I wrote to you."

His hand stops and falls, leaving a chill where his warm touch had soothed me. "I didn't get any letters."

I have to brace myself and gather my composure in order to show him. I don't like that it requires putting any distance between us, but he needs to see this. Shaking off the sadness and putting an end to it, I head to the other end of the kitchen. If I'm ever going to tell him the truth, he has to know that I didn't give up on him. As if I ever could. I never stopped needing him. I just didn't have it in me to face him after what happened.

I didn't deserve him anymore. I still don't.

"I kept the notebooks in a drawer next to the sink." I speak out loud, to drown out my thoughts, and I doubt he can hear me. Sniffling, I reach in and pull out two worn and used-up notebooks. They're nothing special and a number of pages are smudged and crinkled from tears that fell on them during the harder nights.

I present both of them as Cillian stands behind me. Turning to him, I put them in his hands. "I wrote something to you every night." My words are barely a murmur, my tone somber.

He opens the first and closes it quickly. "Why'd you stop coming? Is that in here?"

I shake my head. It's not. I can't even look him in the eye.

He opens it back up.

I don't know what he'll find. I can't remember what I said when I wrote to him, but I remember how I felt. I confided in those pages because it was the only way to keep surviving without him. The notebooks would hold my emotions and I'd be able to go about my life.

Every night, I wrote something down about Cill that I missed, or something I wanted him to know.

It was the only way to keep him from haunting my dreams. I had sound nights and even dreams sometimes when I wrote to him. If I forgot, I'd wake up in a cold sweat from a nightmare. I know that sounds crazy. It's true. I bite the inside of my cheek to keep from telling him that, because I know it sounds ridiculous.

I can't help reading them upside down as Cill skims the entries. I never truly thought I'd get to experience this moment. There was always a chance I wouldn't see his eyes moving over the page and his hands holding the edges of the notebook so carefully.

Sept 5

We went to get our palms read today and I remember the groove on your palm that's split. You remember how I showed you that one time? When Missy showed me how to do palm readings? I think you might have believed her, even if you pretended to be skeptical. I miss her. I miss the club. I miss you the most and I was thinking about that groove. She said that when the lifeline groove is split it means there's going to be an uncertain time. Do you remember that? Do you think that's what this is? It's only a moment that's uncertain? 'Cause if it is, I'm ready for it to end, Cill. I miss you. I miss you so fucking much. I don't know how to make it right, though. I wish I could hold your hand right now. I hope you feel it. Even if I'm too fucking chickenshit to call you or go to you ... I hope you can feel me holding your hand. I love you.

Sept 6

Today was really hard. I think it's my karma. I deserve it. If I'm honest with you, I'm really struggling and I'm lonely and I don't really know what to do, Cill. I didn't get the job at Mac's Hardware. I don't know where else to apply. I don't know what to do, and I want to call you so damn bad, because I know you'd know. You always know, Cill. But if I hear your voice ... I just can't. I can't do this anymore. I'm too damn sad all the time. Can't we just go back? I wish we could just go back and we'd never gone to the club that night. I wish the car had broken down. I wish a storm had flooded the street.

I hate the club. I hate what they did to you. I hate my father. I hate them all. All but you and Reed.

My eyes are ripped from the page as Cill speaks and closes the notebook. It's only then that I realize the emotion in his gaze.

"They should have taken care of you." His voice is deathly low.

Before I can even speak, the breath stolen from my lungs, he continues, "I went away, taking the fall for them and they knew who you were to me."

"Cill—" I start to argue that they did in a way. For a moment they pretended at least, but he cuts me off.

"No, you weren't okay and where the fuck were they?"

"Reed was—" I swallow the words and instead place both palms on Cill's chest as he drops the notebooks to the counter. It takes everything I have to steady my breathing.

"We'll go," Cill states. "The two of us."

"What?" I whisper.

"The clubhouse. It's time for you to go back."

"Things changed when you went away." My voice shakes a little. Lots of things have changed. One that's irrefutable is that I left that world. I don't belong there anymore.

"I said we're going."

"Cill—" Anxiousness overwhelms me. "I don't—"

"Do you work today?" he questions.

"No." I shake my head with the whispered word.

"Good," he says with finality, tapping the notebooks on the counter once before turning his back to me and heading toward the stairs, both books still firmly in his grip. "Get dressed. We're going."

CHAPTER 8

CILLIAN

Which happened first, she left me or the club left her to fend for herself?

My text goes unanswered. Reed saw it, though; it's marked as seen. He's my best friend. Betrayal ran deep during the drive over as I constantly checked to be sure he hadn't responded. I grew up in the life of loyalty and family.

Where the fuck was that for me? Where was it for Kat? She's not the one who betrayed the club. We were kids at best. My father's words scream at me as I recall that night.

He begged me to run, to be anywhere but on the scene when the cops arrived. I should have listened to my old man. Regret is a bitch but betrayal ... it's unforgivable in this world.

The entire way to the club, Kat was silent and if I pressed

a subject, she'd only give me one-word answers. She was too busy picking at the sleeves of her burgundy sweater and a hole in her torn skinny jeans. She was too busy avoiding me and the conversation.

My leather jacket was laid in the back seat of her car and I left it there.

Being home is nothing like I thought it would be. There's a constant anxiousness that has me on edge. Even as I drove Kat's car, taking her back here to the club, I struggled with reaching out to hold her hand.

There's a part of me that's dead and gone. And a part that's mourning what used to be. More than anything I want it back, but as her pace slows with us nearing the club, I question what it used to be. What loyalty meant and whether or not it ever existed.

It hit hard when Kat asked if we were taking my bike.

The dreams of her on the back of my bike carried me through hell and yet, I couldn't bring myself to do it. Not for this.

None of this feels right. It's not what I was told it was. It's as if I've been living a lie. It's eerie as I slip my fingers through her hand and walk through the same door that led to our end four years ago.

"Cillian?" My name on Kat's lips holds fear, insecurity and the threat of her turning around and leaving me as I push open the door.

She pulls back, her boots stumbling in the gravel and her hand leaving mine.

"Don't you dare leave me," I say and the words leave me before I'm able to stop them. With my pulse pounding in my ears, I tell her with a gravelly tone, "You are mine."

Her hazel eyes peer back with more concern than I anticipated, more fear, like it'll kill her to go back to what used to be our home, our haven, the place of nearly all our firsts. "Cill, please," she begs me in a whisper, and it's my undoing.

With one hand wrapping under her thigh and the other on her waist, I lift her up in a swift movement and brace her back against the wall, capturing her lips and reminding her who she belongs to. Even if neither of us will say it out loud. I love her. I need her.

And this hell the club put her through? Seeing her write that she hated the club and feeling deep down that I do too? I can't fucking stand it.

It only takes my lips on hers for my little hellcat to mold her lips to mine. To part the seam of them and grant me entry. Although I'm hard with my kiss at first, my touch softens, her body heats and soft moans pour from her like they used to.

It's only once I'm satisfied she won't run that I pull back and stare into the haze of emotions in her gorgeous eyes.

"The club had no right to leave you." All I keep thinking today, the one thought that won't stop demanding to be heard, is that she would have stayed with me if only they did what the club stands for. If only they'd protected her. She was more mine than she was her father's daughter. She was supposed to be my wife, my everything. "They should have stayed by you until I was out."

A concoction of emotion swirls in her green and gold eyes that I can't place. "I don't know that that's true."

"I do." There's not a second of hesitation. "They knew what you meant to me. Every single one of them." They knew I was going to propose. They all fucking knew. "And that's enough. Do you hear me?"

She nods, swallowing thickly as I slowly lower her to stand on her own, her back still against the old brick wall of the club.

"They need to accept you because you're mine," I tell her firmly and the lack of her denying that is what fuels me to say and do whatever the fuck I have to in order to make this right.

"I am," she murmurs, her gaze still captured in mine.

This time when I gather her hand, she holds it back, walking beside me as I push open the door and lead the way past the garage and upstairs to the rec room.

"Cillian?" my uncle calls out when he first sees me. Standing by the pool table, a whiskey glass in hand, there's not a billiard ball in sight because some kind of plans are laid out on the table. He's quick to gather them, as if they're not for me to see. "You're early," he adds, his voice dropping and his gaze lowering to land on Kat. His nondescript tee and worn jeans are at odds with how I remember this place. It feels empty and cold.

"And you brought company," he states and his voice drops even lower.

Heat blazes across my skin. "Yeah, church isn't for another hour," Finn calls out from the other side of the room. Unlike my uncle, Finn's got his leathers on as well as a pair of reading glasses and a yellow legal pad.

"We're just going over the numbers, something's off," Finn adds, his Irish accent thick, and then sets the pad down on the kitchen counter. It's all the same in this place. The same but older; less thrilling, less wanting.

Is that what they're doing? The fucking accounting?

"Where is everyone?" I call out. It's Sunday so the garage is closed, but this place ... it was never empty. There was always someone here. Footsteps echo down from the stairwell to my right in the narrow hall, the one that leads to the third floor. They're fast paced and light, and it doesn't take long for Reed to come into view.

His expression not at all surprised, and very much carrying the guilt of what my last message said to him.

"You should probably wait for church to start ..." My uncle's voice gathers my attention, "... so you can find your place."

My teeth grind as I take a step forward, Kat protesting slightly as I pull her in behind me.

"You get my message?" I question Reed, who stalks in

after us, carefully following.

"Yeah, I got it," he answers, his glance moving between myself and Kat. They share a look and it's one I don't fucking like.

"Maybe we should go?" Kat asks as I walk to the right of the hall. To the left is the pool table, the television and a sofa which is new and takes up the depth of the room. To the right is the kitchen and before that, the dinner table.

Ignoring Kat, I count the seats and then glance up at my uncle to say, "How many are coming to dinner?"

"Cill–" Kat starts, raising a hand but Reed stops her, murmuring softly, "It's okay." I don't have time to react to them as my uncle answers, "The same as always. Ten."

"We'll need to make that eleven," I state and then stalk to the back where two armchairs with old rubbed leather are seated under the windows.

Snatching one of them, I drag it across the room to make eleven chairs around the table. "I hadn't realized Kat stopped coming, but that mistake has been rectified," I call out across the empty room. It's maybe fifty feet from my uncle to me, but there's not a damn thing that separates the tension.

In only hours all the patched men will be upstairs in the office for church and after that, it's Sunday dinner with all our families. Or that's how it used to be.

Ten.

The number is so damn low.

When did the club dwindle to that? It's not until the legs of the chair are under the table that it hits me. There used to be nine in church alone.

What the fuck happened?

"I can go," Kat speaks and Reed silently watches her.

"You're not going."

As she stares back at me wide eyed and Reed glances between the two of us, the only thing that races through my mind is that I should be the one leading church. I was lined up to be president.

"We need to talk," I announce to my uncle and he's silent, his deep brown eyes boring into mine. I add, "When are we talking?"

"With her here?" the prick dares to question.

Agitation wars with my common sense and anger bristles within me.

"Cillian, calm down." Kat's voice is meek, so unlike her.

"Calm down, man. Let's talk," Reed adds. All the while, my uncle only watches. Finn does the same although it's different. Finn has the decency to look confused and lost. His hands raise and he asks what's going on. He doesn't know what's wrong and that's obvious.

My uncle does, though.

"I left and you turned your back on her," I say, then look my best friend in the eye and he stares back at me like I've sucker punched him.

"It's not like that, and you know it."

Just as I make my move toward Reed there's a crash downstairs from the door being thrown wide open and a deep voice I don't recognize bellows, "We have a warrant to search the premises!" The stairwell of this old place is narrow and the four cops who climb the stairs show one by one, guns pulled and at the ready. Three men, one woman, and none of them look friendly to me.

My heart pounds as I take them in, knowing full damn well I'm on probation and that there's a gun in the waistline of my pants.

Fuck, fuck, fuck.

"What the fuck?" Finn roars from behind me, and Reed takes Kat by the shoulders, pulling her back as the cops enter. Two continue up the stairs and two stand in the doorway as we each raise our hands in the air.

"We're unarmed," Finn tells the two male officers at the same time the pres questions, "Warrant for what, exactly?"

I can't stop staring at Kat. I'm about to lose her again. In the same goddamn place I did years ago, and she didn't want to come in here. She didn't want to do it.

Fuck, I fucking hate myself. Heat flows over my skin. Reed's look of shock must match my own.

Poor Kat stares up at me as I walk quietly to her with eyes full of terror that dart to my waistline. She knows all too well I never leave unarmed. You never know, in this life, when you might need it. Especially when you're fresh out of prison with blood on your hands.

After a round of clears the officers lower their weapons. The two upstairs slowly make their way down.

Uncle Eamon holds an expression of near annoyance. "The fuck is this?" he asks and snatches the warrant from the tallest of officers who holds it out. They're all dressed in their blues and make their way in just as Kat backs up and presses her back into my chest, like she can hide me from them.

My poor hellcat. Regret won't let go of me as it continues to bury itself deep down.

With both of my hands steadying her shoulders, I'm prepared to tell her I love her and I'm sorry. To whisper it into her ear as the officers ask for identification for each of us and Finn argues that we don't have to give them that.

Instead I'm met with her hand, reaching up my back and then into my waistband. I struggle to keep a straight face as she takes the gun.

"Unless the warrant–"

"It's a search and seizure and includes the persons of any Cavanaugh East club members who are on the premises," the cop who seems to be leading the pack announces clear enough for all of us to hear. Kat quietly slips the gun into her purse and stills, with the top flap of it open as the officers approach us.

"I assume that includes everyone here?" he questions,

taking a moment to look each one of us in the eye.

"You're his son, aren't you?" the officer asks me, the skin between his eyebrows wrinkling as he narrows his eyes at me.

"Who do you mean?" *His son.* Anger boils inside of me, this prick bringing up my father when he's long gone.

"The founder of the club, Ronan Cavanaugh."

"Yeah, I'm his son."

"I figured, you look just like him." His gaze moves to Kat and every muscle in my body tightens. "And you?"

"She's my girlfriend. I don't imagine the warrant includes who we're fucking, does it?" I ask as I lay a hand on her shoulders, moving closer, and closing the flap at the same time as I step forward to muffle the noise.

"I'll start with you then?" the officer says. He's got a hard jaw and a clean shave, unlike his partner, whose beard is neatly trimmed and who calls over Reed. Reed stands with his arms out and we both allow the officers to do their job. All the while I watch Reed, who keeps looking at my uncle, who's waiting his turn for the pat down as the other officers search this floor of the club.

With my own hands held out, the officer frisks me, then grabs my wallet and calls in my ID. I know he can't arrest me; I don't have shit on me, but I don't know what the hell is in the club. There shouldn't be a damn thing here.

As if reading my mind, Reed glances up at me and shakes his head, letting me know we're safe as the officer calls in our names, asking if there are any warrants for arrest. Fucking prick.

"There's nothing here," Finn states as he takes the paper from the pres and then flicks it. "Fucking harassment from the DA. Search whatever the fuck you'd like, then get the hell out."

Although the three of us are silent, Finn doesn't let it go. "The hell is this about, anyway?"

"We received an anonymous tip," the lone woman officer answers, standing in the doorway. Her makeup is minimal, her hair pulled back into a tight bun at the base of her neck.

I don't recognize any of these faces. Not from growing up, when I had plenty of run-ins with the law. And not from that fucking night four years ago.

It doesn't take long for the officer to hand back my wallet and ID.

"You okay?" Kat whispers, breaking up my thoughts. Her arm wraps around my waist as she presses herself into me, her grip tight like she refuses to let me go.

"There's nothing here, Daniels," an officer speaks across the room to the head officer in charge. His voice is low and I can't help but note that it was damn fast that they searched. It's almost like they were told where to look. And whatever it was, wasn't there.

"Keep looking." The officer lets out a long exhale, giving out more commands. It's quiet as we stand in silence, watching the men of the law make chaos of the rec room, searching through every cabinet, ripping up every cushion.

They don't leave any inch unturned.

"Church is canceled until further notice," the pres, my uncle, says beneath his breath, his eyes focused on the officer leading the charge, Daniels.

"Yeah," Finn confirms as the rev of motorcycle engines can be heard pulling up to the garage.

Reed's busy texting away, most likely warning whoever it is who showed up at the same time an officer takes the stairs down two by two.

CHAPTER 9

KAT

The kettle whistles angrily and even as I hear it, I don't.

The heavy feel of that gun in my hand consumes my thoughts until I snap out of it. It's been hours, but the tension lingers.

It always seems like a good idea to go back to the kitchen. You can count on things there. Even when life seems unstable, most kitchens have the basics. A sink, a countertop, and a humming fridge. That's where I go when we get back to the house. It helps that there's usually alcohol in the kitchen too.

It's been silent between us since we left. Apart from him kissing my hair and the occasional touches, he hasn't done anything but think. I can practically see the thoughts that wind in his head.

There's a rat. Someone tipped them off and I don't know what exactly the tip was, but I know I could have lost Cill again. All over a fucking gun. All over the fucking club.

Biting down on my lip, I check my phone again.

He didn't say a word to Reed and neither did I when the cops said we were free to leave, much to their chagrin after hours of searching. The expression on Reed's face haunts me and the fact that he didn't respond to my text only makes me worry more.

All I asked him was if he was okay. I know he saw the text, but he hasn't answered.

As I pour the boiling water into the mug, eager for a cup of mint tea to calm my nerves, Cill gets up abruptly, leaving the wooden legs of the kitchen chair to scratch against the floor as he does. He goes upstairs, his footsteps heavy.

"You all right?" I call after him.

"Fine, I'll be back," he answers.

His footsteps keep going. I listen to every one of them. My chest is tight with emotion. He's anything but fine. All of this is fucked. Hating all of it, every last bit of today, I lean against the counter next to the stove and pull out my phone to text Lydia.

Kat: We went to the club. There was a raid.

She texts back right away. Thank God.

Lydia: Oh my god. The cops came?

Kat: Yeah.

Lydia: Are you guys okay? What the hell happened.

Kat: Yeah. As good as we can be. I almost tell her *wrong place, wrong time* jokingly, but I can't do it. I can't make light of what happened.

The cops came, and this time, they didn't take Cill.

Kat: It all feels like a lie.

Lydia: What lie?

Kat: That it was ever safe. That I ever belonged. That I was ever a part of it, a real part. I thought Cill was part of it too. I never thought they'd let him take the fall like that.

With a shaky hand, I put down my phone and breathe deep. The tea is next. I focus on it even as the phone beeps with another text. I harbor so much anger toward all of them. Even to his father who's long gone. Cill never should have taken the fall.

Inhaling the calming tea, I pray for all of them to get what they deserve. After a moment, I'm able to check my phone again.

Lydia: I never thought it was right.

I'm too wrapped up in my thoughts to hear Cill come back down, so he's able to catch me off guard as his arms fold around me the next second.

"Hey, Hellcat." His tone is calmer than it's been all day, which instantly soothes me. It doesn't go unnoticed that we were tense around each other earlier, but after what happened at Cavanaugh Crest, he hasn't stopped touching me.

I couldn't be more grateful. I need him to be steady for me. "You okay?"

"No," I admit. The back of my throat is tight. I'm not on the verge of breaking down, but I'm angry. "There's so much that's just fucking wrong." The bitterness lingers after the words are spoken. A part of me expects him to deny the reality, like my father used to do, but he doesn't and that's all the more shocking.

"I know," he answers in a whisper. He adds, "I'm going to make it all right. I promise," and I wish he wouldn't.

How could he promise such a thing? It's all fucked. I catch my bottom lip between my teeth before it trembles and Cill looks me in the eye, the comfort changing to something else. Something darker and something more sinful.

"You're going to need a safe word, Kat."

My head tilts immediately to the floor, thinking of the phrase my father gave me and hating it, hating him. The rage is instantly subdued as Cill grabs my chin between his thumb and forefinger, bringing my attention back to him as he tells me, "So when I whip your ass for taking my gun, I'll know if I'm going too hard on you."

"Cillian," I murmur, my eyes widening with shock but my body heating with anticipation.

"Word, my little hellcat," he commands, his voice still soothing even as the threat of punishment looms.

"Mulberry," I speak without thinking. Mulberry is the

street where an old pizzeria used to sit on the corner. Cillian first "punished" me behind that pizzeria.

It wasn't much of a punishment if you ask me, getting fucked raw while he played with my ass. A tingle heats my skin at the memory.

He smirks at the word, maybe knowing exactly why I picked it, but it falls as quickly as it came to grace his lips. "You aren't going to do that again, do you understand?"

"Yes." Although the answer is instant, my internal agreement is not. For him, I'd do it all again. If I can protect him in any way, I will.

There's no way I could stand by and watch like I did before. I couldn't live with myself if I did.

"I mean it, Kat," he murmurs and I wonder if he knows what I'm thinking. "If they took you away, I ... I don't know what I would do." His voice is tight with emotion.

Cill holds me tighter and kisses my cheek, then my lips. It's far softer than he's been with me since he's come home.

As he pulls me in closer, my front to his, I can feel how hard he is. It ignites every nerve ending instantly.

"Being apart from you has been hell," he murmurs against my lips before kissing me again. My hands slip up his shirt to his bare shoulders, eager to touch him.

He lets his hands roam over my body, and when I don't pull away, he starts pulling at my clothes. One by one he strips them off until I'm naked. The chill of the air dancing along my skin as if it's part of the foreplay.

"Stay facing the counter," he says, his hands reaching down to unbuckle his belt.

I obey, the warmth between my thighs clenching with a new heat and desire.

In the reflection of the kitchen window, which thankfully faces an empty field that leads to woods so it's all shades of dark moss and sage, I watch as he pulls his shirt over his head, his muscles rippling. Then he steps closer to me again and arranges my hands on the sides of the counter.

The leather of his belt sings as it's pulled through the loops of his jeans. A shiver rolls down my shoulders and it's immediately halted by Cill's strong grip. His thumb travels in a soothing stroke up to the base of my neck and back down with each word.

"If I ever scare you, I want you to tell me."

His somber tone is unexpected, given the predicament.

"I'm not scared of you, I'm scared of ..." I start to say as his expression reaches mine in the reflection, "... losing you, but also everything that comes with being with you again."

"But you are with me."

"Yes," I answer eagerly. It's only then that I realize how deeply I mean it. Even if he doesn't know what happened. Maybe I'll never have to tell him. It doesn't matter, does it? If I love him like this. If I'm willing to do whatever he wants?

"Good because I can't lose you again," he says and then his

head falls to the crook of my neck. His grip on my shoulder loosens as he plants a kiss on the tender spot below my ear. My eyes close and my nipples pebble as he drags the edge of the leather down the curve of my side.

"Then don't leave me," I beg him.

"I won't leave you, so long as you don't leave me."

"I won't. I promise," I tell him in a desperate rush.

Brushing my hair to the side, he kisses my neck and whispers, "That's my good girl" before pulling back, leaving only his left hand gripping my shoulder.

"You need to obey, though, my little hellcat," he says as his tone darkens and I nod, knowing what's coming.

"Count to three for me," he says and before I can agree, the first lash lands across my ass.

I hiss in a breath, seething as he massages the mark with the palm of his hand, kneading my heated flesh.

"Count," he reminds me, his lips at my ear and then he kisses my cheek as I breathe out the word, "One."

"Good girl."

Two and three come back-to-back, leaving my lips parted as the stinging pain makes my toes curl. Before I can even exhale, his fingers find my clit and he rubs ruthless circles.

"Two and three," I murmur as I bend over the sink, holding on to it to keep me upright.

"Good girl," he says, complimenting me again in that deep, soothing tone of his.

I love it. I love this.

Cill eases my feet apart with one of his and strokes between my legs. Ruthlessly and demanding my desire. As I moan, his left hand grips the globe of my ass, bringing a heated sensation of pain that heightens the pleasure.

With my teeth sinking into my bottom lip, I give in to the need to mewl as the waves threaten to crash around me, drowning me in the sinful need.

The sensation pulls tight in the pit of my stomach and then rages outward, paralyzing me and all the while, Cill plays with my body, kissing along my exposed neck and plucking my nipples at a whim.

Once my orgasm has peaked, he pulls my hips toward him so that he can angle himself to my opening and push inside. I let out another soft moan, reaching for something to grip as he fucks me deeply and without mercy.

"Damn, you feel like fucking heaven," he says low into my ear. "You feel just like I remember. My first and only."

His words force me to tense. I'm not how I always was. And he's no longer my only. Cill's not the only one I've been with. I wish we'd had the kind of life where we could have stayed together. I wish I wasn't carrying around this guilt. He fucks me with even strokes while that horrible guilt fills up my lungs.

"It's all right, Hellcat," he says like he already knows.

My voice is thick with unspoken secrets. "I don't know if it is, Cill." Does he know? Please, let him know. Let him know and still love me regardless. *Please still love me.*

He doesn't stop. Instead he reaches around in front of me and circles my clit with a fingertip.

"You can tell me whatever you want," he says gruffly.

Pleasure builds between my legs. My head thrashes with the undeniable heat.

"How am I supposed to tell you things if—if they'll ruin this moment?"

He takes a deep breath and lets it out, pulling nearly all the way out and then slamming back into me, my hips butting against the edge of the counter, nearly bruising.

"I'm inside you," he says finally. "It's where I wanted to be every goddamn day for the last four years. You can tell me whatever the fuck you want, and it won't ruin a damn thing." He doesn't stop and the pleasure doesn't let up. Neither does the burning secret begging to spill from me.

He thrusts into me slowly as he tells me, "I want you and I'll never stop wanting you."

Kisses greet my side, his hands roaming along my sensitized skin. It's all too much. His touch is gentle and it strips down the boundaries I've been holding around myself. I can't tell him the whole story. I'm not ready, and neither is he.

"I'll ask you questions," he says, stroking in and out of me steadily. "How about that?"

I'm barely able to utter a word, but I agree, nodding my head as the pleasure rises. He grips my ass as he thrusts in deeper and harder.

"How many men were you with while I was away?" he questions and my eyes open wide, my heart thumping in fear of being torn to shreds. "Don't lie to me, Hellcat."

Only a moment passes. All the while, he keeps up his pace. With my breath unsteady I answer him. "One," I say.

He swallows hard, so hard I can hear it, and I think he might drop it until he asks, "Did he treat you right?"

Every thrust forces my hips to hit the counter and heat engulfs me as I nod.

"I'm sorry," I say, the tears falling, the pleasure and the pain intertwined. "I'm sorry, Cill."

He pulls out of me and I almost crumple across the countertop. *No. No, please. Don't leave me.* The words are trapped at the back of my throat, and they're kept there by Cill's bruising kiss. He turns me to face him and lifts me up to perch on the edge of the counter. Then he thrusts himself inside of me and braces my back with his forearms as he fucks me like he always has. Possessively and with a passion that's undeniable.

I bury my head in the crook of his neck, my warm breath suffocating me as I realize what I've just told him.

"Look at me, Hellcat."

Sharp blue eyes pierce through me and hold me in place as he takes from me. It's a punishing fuck, hard and deep.

All the while, I struggle between the push and pull of pleasure and pain, praying he doesn't ask me who.

CHAPTER 10

CILLIAN

She has a way of calming me. I swear to God the last year in that hell was unbearable because she left me. Every time I think back on it all I know is that my father passed, we had an argument and then things changed.

Staring down at the texts from Reed, that began last night until this morning, I know I should be focused on the club, but I want answers from my hellcat.

Why is she so fucking scared now, walking into the club like she doesn't belong?

What happened—what really fucking happened that drove her away? Was it me? Or was it something else ... was it someone else?

Reed (7:14 pm): You two all right?

Reed (8:09 pm): The police just came knocking now.

Reed (8:10 pm): They haven't stopped since you left. Every couple of months there's something.

Reed (10:26 pm): Can we talk?

Reed (10:47 pm): Can you at least let me know that you're still fucking alive and they didn't arrest you again?

Reed (11:14 pm): I just drove by her place and talked to Lydia. Look, I'm sorry. When your pops left, and Eamon took over, things changed. In a lot of ways and I wish they didn't but we have to talk.

Reed (9:15 am): I think there's a rat. I think whoever it is either wants you back in jail or they were after me this time. I was moving supplies when you came in. I only put it back and stopped because I heard your voice downstairs. If you hadn't come just then, I would've been holding it. I wouldn't have had a chance to hide the shit.

Cillian (9:15 am): Delete that shit right now.

Reed (9:16 am): Then let me come over. Fucking talk to me.

Cillian (9:18 am): Come over

The rustling by the sink brings my attention up to Kat. The morning light kisses her face through the kitchen window as she rinses off the pan. Her hips sway as she dries it. I must be addicted to her, because even with the world crashing down around us, all I want to do is lay her on the table and fuck her until she comes undone with my name on her lips.

"Reed's coming over," I speak out loud, if for no other

reason than one of us will know we have company soon and I can't strip her down unless we want to get caught.

Her hair falls down her shoulder, exposing the thin strap to her satin nightie. "Right now?" she questions in a breathy voice and it's only then I realize she may want to change. The fabric is thin and as my gaze drops to her chest, I note her nipples are pebbled.

"Yeah, you may want to change," I comment as I lift the cup of coffee to my lips. I'm not given a chance to take a sip, though.

The knock at the front door is followed immediately with him opening it. "It's me," he calls out before shutting it. We can only hear him as I answer that we're in the kitchen.

When he comes into view, it's obvious he didn't sleep for shit. His clothes are rumpled and the bags under his eyes add to the pathetic demeanor. The sight of him is exactly what women must see when they say he looks like a lost puppy.

"Hey." Reed's greeting is complete with a nervous swallow. My entire body tenses but I tell him hey in return. I don't know if the man standing in front of me is my best friend or a fucking traitor.

He glances at Kat and respectfully averts his gaze to me, leaving her standing in the corner of the kitchen as he takes the closest seat which puts him straight across from me at the table and her at his left.

"You want coffee?" Kat asks and Reed nods, his gaze

focused on the wilting flowers in the center of the table. With a deep breath in he gets right to the point. "It had to be a setup."

"Who? Who would have even known I was heading in?"

"It could have been me they were setting up," Reed offers but then hesitantly looks over his shoulder at Kat, still standing in the corner of the kitchen by the sink. Watching silently.

"Back when Missy—"

"Don't bring up her name," I say, cutting him off as my voice drops deathly low. Just the mention of Missy, a woman who was like a second mother to me, the woman who kept the club together and then ratted, makes my blood boil.

Reed is silent, staring back at me like he has something to say. He doesn't say a word, though. "Who could be the leak? Who's the rat now?"

"They're saying it's Kat, but I don't think it is."

"Who the fuck is saying it's her?"

"Me?" Kat's tone echoes both disbelief and fear. "I wouldn't dare," she says, barely getting out the choked words.

"Who the fuck said it's Kat?" I say harsher, slamming my fist down to get their attention.

Reed looks me dead in the eye when he tells me, "Your uncle."

"Fucking hell," I say, gritting the words between clenched teeth. Everything runs cold and I look up at Kat to find her expression fallen and true fear in her gorgeous eyes.

"I'll kill them before they think to say that shit again ... let alone touch you."

"It's not her," Reed says and then glances up at Kat to add, "I know it's not you. We all know you wouldn't."

"Then why the fuck was her name even mentioned?" The cords in Reed's throat tighten as he swallows. "Is it because of her father?" I ask, my anger barely contained. Before I can help myself, before Reed can even answer, my decision to go back there is final. Leaning over the table, I stare down Reed and ask, "How did you let this happen?"

"I think maybe you should calm—"

As my fist slams down on the table, I can feel the rage boiling. I've always had anger issues, my pops used to say I was temperamental. Prison only made that worse.

"They turned their backs on her the moment I left." I still have the ring I was going to give her. The memory of it only makes the pain worse. "It's a betrayal and it needs to be dealt with."

"Cill, it's—"

"We're going back," I say and my tone holds no room for negotiation as I meet each of their gazes. It doesn't escape me that there's worry buried inside each of them. When did conversations about the club get met with fear? "We're going back." It takes everything in me to keep my voice calm and lower it to add, "We're going to do another vote and I'm going to put it all back to the way it was."

Even as the words leave me, I know it'll never be what it once was. If that's what I want, the family the club used to be, I might as well start over.

That very thought echoes in Reed's eyes.

"They don't want me in there and that's fine. But I would never–" Seeing my hellcat give in, seeing her cower under the idea of going back ... I fucking lose it.

"It's not fine! Who the fuck said they don't want you there? My uncle?"

"Calm down, Cillian."

"It's my fucking club," I scream, my muscles coiling.

"My father's," I add and my voice splits with emotion I have no fucking intention of dealing with. "I should have been there," I shout, each word emphasized with the slamming of my fist.

"How could they make you feel like you weren't welcome?" I say and stare down Kat, my everything. Her eyes are glossy and I can't fucking take it.

"Reed, how could you let this happen!" I'm met with nothing but silence, both of them staring at me like they would a wild, uncaged animal. "I should fucking kill him ..."

"No one's killing anyone right now, Cill. Man, you just got out," Reed points out, attempting to temper my anger.

"I need you to calm down so I can tell you—" Kat does the same, although she doesn't finish.

"Tell me what?"

"When I ... when we stopped ..." My hellcat grips the counter as if she needs it to hold her up. "I was with someone and your uncle found out, and that's why."

"So fucking what? So what if you slept with someone. That's between us. It's none of his fucking business." I don't care that she fucked someone. I care that he wasn't good enough to keep her and that she's mine now. That's all that matters. My uncle can go to hell if he doesn't like it.

"Cill ... it's who."

"Who? Who was it?"

"I think you should calm down," Reed offers, no longer sitting as he steps away from the table.

"I have to tell him. I have to, Reed," she says and Kat's shoulders crumple on his name. What the fuck is going on.

Who could make her break down? My hellcat. I only survived that first year because of her. What the hell is going on?

"Cillian, just sit down, man." Reed glances to Kat, his agony in her pain ... I finally put two and two together.

It's a bullet to the chest. Shocking and paralyzing as I realize it was Reed.

"Was it you?" I manage, the words sounding heavy and deep as the room blurs and all I can see is my best friend's face.

"You fucked her and dropped her," I speak the reality out loud. It was him ... and he let the club drop her? He let her turn into this weak version who's more afraid than I've ever seen her.

"You did this to her?" My body's heavy as I stand, the legs of the chair scraping against the floor as I straighten my back.

"No, it wasn't like that," Reed insists, taking a hesitant step away from both Kat and myself.

Kat's apologies are drowned out by him telling me to calm down.

"You fucked her?" I ask although they've already admitted it. Denial and betrayal bring my hand to form a fist, the skin across my knuckles stretched so tight they turn white.

With a single glance down, Reed's hands fall to his side, resigned to the fact he's about to get the karma he's had coming.

I get one in, one solid punch before he yells out something incoherent and as I go in for another, purely fueled by rage, he slams his fist into my jaw, the crack and blister of pain barely registers.

Just like I can hardly hear Kat's scream.

KAT

"You don't understand. It wasn't like that," Reed tries to explain as if Cill's in any state to listen.

"She was mine! Mine and you were supposed to protect her."

I beg him, "You're scaring me Cillian, please! Please! Stop!" I can't get out the words: they have to stop yelling.

The cops can't come.

"Stop," I cry out, watching the two of them barreling their fists at each other's faces. Reed throws his weight into Cillian and the two of them slam into the kitchen table. It gives instantly, splintering between the two of them as they crash onto the floor.

Make it stop.

"Please! Cillian, let go!" Reed's attempt to back away is denied. Cillian's hell-bent on getting his anger out and as much as I can't blame him, I can't let it happen.

He can't go to jail.

"Please, Cillian," I cry out again and as they scream at each other, their voices getting louder and louder, I act without thinking. My body wraps around Cillian's back, my arms over his shoulders and my legs around his waist, my face buried in his neck.

Everything is hot and turmoil rages inside of me as I beg him to stop, knowing it's all my fault. I did this.

"Off me, Kat! Get off before you get hurt!"

"Run, Reed!"

Cillian's hands wrap around my arms as he grits between his teeth, "Off, Kat. Get off before you get hurt."

It's enough time to give Reed the chance to get out of the rubble and the moment I see his feet steady on the ground I yell out for him to leave. "Get out! Go!"

Cill attempts to stand but my weight throws him off and he staggers back, falling and my shoulder bashes against the cabinet.

"You're protecting Reed!" Incredulity is clear in his voice and for the first time in my life, I'm afraid of him.

"Please! Please! Mulberry." My world spins and my body trembles pressed tightly against Cillian's hard body. "Mulberry," I whisper again and hate myself. "Please, Cillian. Please."

"Let go of me, Kat." His voice is lowered as the front door shuts. But I can't let go yet. I have to give Reed time. Unable to speak, I shake my head.

"I need you to let me go." Betrayal sinks into his words.

"I can't, Cillian. Please. Please just ... I can't."

CHAPTER 11

KAT

My hands won't stop shaking, not even as I clean up the chunks of glass and the shards of ceramic from the debris left behind from Reed and Cill's fight.

The table's broken and Cill's face is already bruised on the right side across his sharp jawline. Tears spill silently as I clean up the mess, attempting any semblance of sanity.

"I'm sorry," I repeat in a whisper as I pull my legs into my chest, leaning against the counter and feeling the cold against my heated cheek.

Everything happened too quickly, far too quickly and it's at odds with how slow and long the last four years have been.

More importantly, everything is broken. It was always the three of us and when Cill went away, time shredded any chance of us staying the same.

Cill's hands run through his hair as he paces in the threshold.

I'm grateful Reed's gone and they've stopped. I'm grateful Cill knows because he needed to. And that's all I'm grateful for.

I wish I would fucking die right now. Truly, watching the pain Cill's in, I pray for death as I choke on my sobs and apologies.

"I need to ride," he says and I can only nod.

I swallow thickly and agree with him. "Okay," I manage and then the selfish part of me spills out when I say, "Promise me you'll come home."

"You still love me?" he questions as he stands by the broken table, towering over me as I'm on my knees and it's torture that he has to ask.

I did this. I deserve to feel this hell that rages inside of me. The turmoil causes my cheeks to burn.

"Come with me now."

"Cill?"

"I can't stay here. You fucked him here, didn't you?" His words slap across my face and all I can do is nod.

"I don't want my bike right now," he decides, his tone holding no negotiation. "Put on your clothes and get in the car."

I can barely look him in the eye as I push up off the ground and brush past him to get clothes, but he grips me first. His hand lands on my arm and pushes me against the wall.

My back hits the threshold and before I can object, before I can do anything but gasp, his lips are on mine.

My body's reaction is instant, holding him back for dear life. My pulse races and my blood heats.

His kiss is possessive, harsh and brutal. But it's him. He kisses me and I savor it, in case it's the last.

When he stops, he doesn't move anything but his lips away from mine and I stand there breathless and waiting for judgment.

His gaze moves to my shoulder, where there's a small scrape when he asks, "Are you all right?"

Nodding gently, ever so gently so he doesn't move, so he doesn't let me go, I tell him, "I'm fine."

With his forehead pressed against mine he whispers, "Get dressed. Now."

I do as I'm told, quickly dressing to make myself presentable. All the while my thoughts race, the regrets and the raging emotion.

My heart pounds as I make my way downstairs to a waiting Cillian. He gets in my way when I try to take the keys. He doesn't say anything, just pushes past me and gets into the driver's seat.

A minute later we're speeding down the street away from the city and thankfully the opposite direction of the club and Reed's place.

All the while, I glance at a brokenhearted Cillian, hating

that I put that scowl on his face. Hating the bruise that's already marred his stubbled jaw. He barely looks at me and I struggle to speak. To tell him how much pain I was in. How it was a mistake ... but how I fell in love with Reed and needed him.

How I ended it because it was wrong. I ended it with Reed. I ended it with Cillian too.

Cill makes a right, then a left. My heart pumps adrenaline throughout my body. I want to believe it'll turn out okay, but I haven't felt this scared since Cill was arrested.

A gas station comes up on our right. The lights above the pumps are blinding against the night sky.

The corner of the street is nearly dead this time of night. A tire store on one end is closed although the parking lot is packed with the cars of men who are a block down at the strip joint. On the other side is a gas station and the corner store. It's a bit run down but that's the way it is in this city. The lower down the hill, the worse the condition. As you drive up the hill and the blocks go from Twentieth Street up to First Street, the houses are nicer, the parks cleaner.

I think it's the way all old cities are.

"No fucking way," says Cill under his breath. His tone alerts me that something's wrong.

I turn my head and see the parked car. *Fuck. No.*

Before I can stop him Cill pulls over, the brakes screeching. We're facing the wrong direction on the road.

"Please," I cry out, "Cillian, don't!" It's like fate set him up. "He's not worth it," I say as Cill finally stops nose to nose with the parked car. My heart races.

No, no. Please, Cillian. Tears prick at the corners of my eyes.

He's angry and right in front of us is an object of his hatred. Duncan Tray. The fucker who tried to take advantage the moment Cill was locked away and then again when his father passed.

I know the cherry red muscle car is his and as I glance from it to Cill's expression, my chest tightens with a knowing dread.

He's always been a problem for the MC. My father used to tell me to keep a lookout for him. There was a rumor in the club that he gave the police some of the information they used to arrest Cill. I'm certain Cill heard it too.

If nothing else, the guy's a creep and belongs behind bars for that in and of itself.

"Wait. Cill, stop."

He shoulders open the driver's door, leaving the keys in the ignition which sound off in a *beep, beep, beep* as Cill steps out into the street.

I take in the gas station but I don't see Duncan Tray anywhere.

"Cill, please stop," I beg him, managing to get out even though my body's numb.

He doesn't even hesitate as he opens the trunk and I beg him not to.

"I know you're upset. But please, Cill, don't do this."

His shoulders radiate angered power as he palms the tire iron.

"Cill, please ..." I trail off as he closes the trunk with a thud. My vision spins and blurs with the fear of cops being called.

On the first swing, he shatters the driver's side window of the other car.

It shatters and the glass sprays.

"Get in the car, Kat," is all Cillian says before he swings for the back window. His rage has taken over his body.

Cill smashes one of the side mirrors, then the other. He's raining dents down on the body of the car. One foot stomps down on the front bumper and it collapses into the street. The windshield is next. It takes the most effort.

Holy fucking shit.

My pulse is out of control and I can't breathe.

The cops are going to come. They're going to arrest Cill, and he won't get another chance. He's on probation.

"Cill, you have to stop." I raise my voice to be heard over the sound of metal on metal. "Cill. Cillian. The cops are going to come."

He breaks through the rest of the windshield, sending shattered glass flying onto the front seat. I run to his side before he can take another swing. He puts his fist through the broken glass instead. It cuts him. "Stop," I beg him, screaming so loud the words feel as if they're ripped up my throat. "You have to stop."

Cill blinks down at me, his eyes flashing. "No."

"Yes. They're going to arrest you."

I take a big step back, then another. I can't breathe.

"I can't lose you!" I tell him and my body trembles. Glancing across the street, eyes watch us. Fuck. I force my body to move. I can't let them call the cops.

"Where the hell are you going?" He narrows his eyes. I turn around and check the street for traffic, then run across.

Cill follows me across, dropping the lug wrench with a loud clang. His face is red with anger but he's not destroying the car anymore. Not that it matters. The damage is already done.

Just as I get to the glass door, Cill puts his hand on the door and tries to keep it shut. "You're not going in there, Hellcat." Rage still has its grip on him, making him a fucking lunatic.

"Yes I am," I shoot back. I push his hand away.

He's fucking crazy if he thinks we can just drive away and no one will tell. They know who he is and who I am. I have to fix this. I push all my weight against Cillian, screaming *look what you did*, and he seems to snap out of it, only slightly. Enough that I can rip the door open, a bell chiming far too sweetly for the moment.

I have to do something. I can't let him go to jail again. I can't.

The cashier's eyes are wide as I rush up to the checkout. Cill's presence isn't helping anything. He stalks behind me, his hand bleeding. I put both hands on the countertop and swallow thickly.

"Listen to me. Please." My voice is shaken. "I need you to do something for me. I know you have security cameras. I need you to delete the last few minutes of footage. The last ten minutes. That's all I need."

"I can't do that." Her head shakes as she looks from me to Cill with genuine fear.

"It's right behind you," I say as I point and then tell her, "The guy who owns that car hurt a woman in our club years ago. Please." Hearing Cillian move behind me, I turn to see his hand run down the back of his head as he looks out of the doors.

When I look back at the cashier, a young woman, younger than me even with a high ponytail and wide eyes, I beg her, "Please."

"I don't want to get in trouble," she whispers and Cillian's tone of regret can be heard behind me, reality setting in.

"Please," I repeat.

"He went to jail for me, and he can't go back." I suck in a breath, panic setting in. We need to get out of here before Duncan Tray gets here. It's already been too long. Minutes have passed. Cops will be here soon. Fuck. Fuck.

She opens her mouth, and I just know she's not going to do it.

"Please," I beg again. "Look at me and try to understand.

I just need this one thing from you, and I promise you, it'll mean the world to me. It would be everything to me if you deleted this footage."

She swallows thickly. "There are two other stores," she says hesitantly. "I'd have to call around and ask them to do the same thing."

"Do they like you?"

"What?"

"The other people at the stores. Do they like you enough to do it?"

She nods.

"Cill, give me your wallet." My hand shakes as I hold it out to him. I'm praying that nobody else walks in right now. I just need to get us both the hell out of here. Quickly.

Cill digs in his pocket and hands me his wallet. I open it and take out all the cash, sliding it across the countertop to the girl. It's a decent wad. There's got to be a few hundred there.

"Please call them," I say urgently, shoving it across the counter and glancing back at the two cars, one fucked up and then mine which still has the driver's door open. My chest heaves with my chaotic breathing.

She bites her lip and glances out at the pumps. All the while, madness bristles through me.

She disappears into the back room.

"I'm sorry, Hellcat," Cill manages the moment she's gone. My broken man stands by the doors like he knows this is the end.

"I'll fix this. I promise," I tell him with desperation although I can already feel him slipping away. His temper has always gotten the better of him.

Always.

"The last ten minutes didn't happen." I hear her before I hear the door swing open.

Relief floods through me at the same time that I hear sirens wail in the distance.

"I'll call them," she tells me as she reaches for the phone and her face pales. "The cops are going to come here. What do I tell them? The other stores are one thing, but I don't know about the cops."

I look her straight in the eye. "Tell them it was four guys in a Chevy. You got it? Four guys in a Chevy got out, wrecked the car, and drove off."

"I don't know ..."

"The club will have your back." I'm gambling huge by saying this. I'm not part of that group anymore, but I'll go back to them if I have to. "You know who I'm talking about?"

"You sure about that?" she questions, her eyes darting outside.

"I'm sure."

"Okay." She gives me a fast nod. "I got it. Go before they get here."

"Thank you," I barely get out before taking Cill's hand and

tugging him toward the door.

"Fuck, Hellcat," he says, realization of what he risked in his voice. "Fuck, fuck, fuck."

"Come on." We break into a jog outside the gas station. I run around and get into the car on the driver's side. My fingernail catches on the mechanism to adjust the seat and breaks. Cill slides in next to me and I put my foot on the gas. Blue and red lights are just barely seen in the rearview mirror.

"I've got this," I say under my breath. I pull out into the street like we never parked on the wrong side of the road and gently accelerate over the next block. I stop at an intersection, then keep going. As soon as I think it's safe, I make a left turn and keep driving.

If they start looking for us, I don't want to go back to my house. My heart pounds and protests. Everything is at war inside of me. As if today could get any worse.

Headlights in the rearview mirror scare the shit out of me.

"Someone's behind us."

Cill twists around in his seat, the leather groaning as he does. "It's Reed." His voice is thick with emotion.

I'm hanging on by a thread and although I know there's tension, I need Reed. Cillian needs Reed. My words are caught in the back of my throat as I gauge Cill's expression. With an open cut on his hand, blood on his shirt and the bruise on his face, I'm torn to shreds over how broken my first love is.

For years, all I've known is that I couldn't fix anything.

That life was shitty and I didn't trust myself let alone anyone else. It has to change. I have to fix this.

As I take in a steadying breath, I pull off into a public parking area that almost no one uses behind the old strip mall and park.

Cill's swallow is audible as he turns in his seat, staring ahead with a deadly glare.

Reed pulls up next to me. The seat belt clicks as I unlatch it and I take one glance at Cillian before getting out.

Reed follows my lead, and it's the first chance I have to take a good look at him. The cut on his brow is swollen and red and his left cheek sports a bruise that matches Cillian's.

Emotions storm through me. Regret and anguish most of all.

As I heave in a breath, barely standing straight, I feel ragged and shaken. I can barely believe any of the events of today have happened.

Before I can speak a word, Reed states, "You've gotta leave the car, Kat. Don't drive it anymore tonight."

"How do you–Were you following us?"

"No. I got a call from my buddy ... the bodyguard at the strip joint. He saw everything but it's taken care of."

He doesn't look me in the eye and he doesn't look to Cill either. The man in front of me is a man who came out of a debt he owes.

"Are you okay?" I question, feeling the weight of it all.

He offers me a sad smile with the shake of his head, his deep brown eyes echoing a sorrow I know all too well. One of loss and regret. One that's given up but still has to move on.

"Reed–"

He cuts me off. "I'll take you wherever you need to go. Neither of you should be driving right now."

With my eyes locked on his, I wish he could feel everything I feel. I wish he knew everything I'm thinking. For a moment, it feels as if he might.

"I just want to fix this," I whisper but I doubt my words are heard over the sirens that steal our attention.

I turn around and poke my head into the car. "We're going with Reed."

"No we're fucking not," says Cill.

"We need to go to Nello's ... by The Ruin," Reed speaks over me, easily heard by Cillian.

It's a restaurant that has a private back room. It's hours away, in Desolation, New York. Club members go there when they want a private conversation, or to wait out a complicated situation. It's a nice restaurant, fancy even. I certainly can't afford it on my own. That's maybe the best cover of all. People don't think members of the MC would eat at a place with white tablecloths.

"Come on, Cill," I say softly.

"We'll walk," Cill shouts out the window at Reed. "That'll be enough time to get them off our backs. We'll fucking walk there."

"You're not going to walk there like that. I saw you come out of the gas station. I know you're bleeding," Reed answers.

Cill is silent for another long moment, then he curses under his breath and gets out.

I climb into Reed's car first. Cill's still pissed, and I don't blame him. I would be furious and heartbroken. I would be a fucking wreck.

"We just need a place to calm down," Reed says. "We can talk while we're there, man."

"There's nothing you can say."

"I think there is," Reed replies. "I think there are things you need to know. Fuck, Cill. This isn't how I wanted this to play out. I sure as hell know you wanted it different. We all did. Get in the car."

CHAPTER 12

REED

1 YEAR AGO

When I open the door to Kat's place, the first thing I notice is the broken frame in the foyer. My blood spikes with adrenaline as I search for any evidence of a break-in.

"Kat?" I call out her name, attempting to close the door quietly behind me although it creaks.

"In here," her somber voice calls out and I'm given a fraction of a second to feel relief until I hear her crying.

Kicking the door closed, I bypass the broken glass from the destroyed frame and head to the kitchen to find Kat covering her face at the sink. The water's running and when she peeks up at me, her eyes are swollen from crying and her reddened cheeks are tearstained.

"You okay?" Every step I take is careful as I approach her. In satin pink pajamas and without an ounce of makeup on, she's both gorgeous and utterly raw. A primitive side of me wants to console her; another side craves to comfort her in the way I know she needs.

She sniffles and turns off the water, giving me her back as she reaches for the kitchen towel to pat her face dry.

Tossing the towel down she gives me a careless shrug as if she hasn't lost all composure.

"What happened to the picture?"

"I threw it," she admits with feigned strength and then her composure seems to diminish, leading her to confide in me.

"He yelled at me. Like I'm the reason his father died? He just ... he's losing it and I can't help him."

As tears well in her eyes, she grips the counter to hold her balance. "I loved his dad too. What can I do? I don't know what to do."

She loses it, and as she covers her face, turning away from me, I casually approach her. She's wounded and I know the feeling. Cill's father was a second father to me.

His death was sudden and I know Cill's not taking it well.

None of us are.

But he shouldn't yell at her. "He's just angry right now, but he loves you."

"I'm angry too," she sobs. She's anything but angry. She's

broken. Both of them, my two best friends, are nothing like what they used to be.

"It's going to be okay," I whisper, and when I reach out to her, she leans into my touch. At first it's only slightly, but as the grief takes over, she falls into me.

I'm grateful to hold her, to give her this. Because I'm struggling too.

I feel us all falling apart and I don't know how to make it right.

When I kiss the top of her head and whisper into her hair it's going to be all right and that he loves her, I mean it, and I have to stop myself from telling her I love her too ... because at this moment, I know I mean it just the same.

Present time

"I'm not here to fight you." That's the first thing I have to say to Cill, even if it's not quite true. Hell, maybe we are here, in the back room of Nello's, next to The Ruin, to fight. Maybe we're here to have it out. I'd rather have him punch me than some asshole across from the gas station. I won't send him to jail.

My body's still ringing from earlier today in Kat's kitchen, even after the nearly two hours of silent driving to get here. I think we all needed a moment of quiet and time to think. But two hours wasn't enough. I don't know that any amount of time will prepare me for this.

The dim lights in the back room only make Cill's bruised cheek look worse. He'll get over it, just like I will.

My shoulders straighten with barely contained anger as I take in a heavy breath. Although I know the anger isn't justified, it's still there.

I never should have touched Kat, but inside all I can think is that he never should have left us. All of it was fucked.

"I don't want to fight you," I tell him again. "What happened between Kat and me is long over." As I say the words, my heart is in agony. It feels like this is it for all three of us.

I fell in love with Kat, I fell hard for her and I only wanted to love her, because I knew CIll couldn't. It wasn't supposed to happen like it did. I never stopped loving her, though. Just like I never stopped wanting to be the friend Cill needed either.

We were both missing him. Both broken ... hell, all three of us were.

Glancing over at Kat, sitting beside Cill in the circular booth and across from me, I know she'd choose him ten out of ten times. I'm the piece that has to go for them to be together now and it's my fault. I know that, but I can't stand that it has to happen.

Clearing my throat, I face Cill head-on, doing what needs to be done. "You need to know what happened with the club, even if you hate me right now. I want to tell you everything I know."

The stark white tablecloth is gently lit by the candle in the middle of the table, and a basket of bread wrapped in a white cloth napkin to keep it warm separates us.

It's quiet back here and the waiter is more than aware that we need time to discuss business so I doubt we'll see him again until Cill calls for him. With the location so close to The Ruin, Nello's is used to this. They're paid well, even if we don't order a damn thing to eat.

I could confess everything to Cill in this room. Spill every detail and I don't know what will happen after. I dread what will come. But it has to be done.

"What the hell happened to the club?"

"Things changed when your uncle took over."

"You keep saying that." Cill looks me dead in the eye. He's wary of me now and I don't blame him. I would be too if he fucked the love of my life without me knowing. "Tell me the truth, Reed. You owe me that."

It's not always best to tell the truth. Anyone who grew up at the Cavanaugh Crest knew that. Sometimes it's best to keep your damn mouth shut. Everybody loves to talk about how honesty is the best policy, but it's bullshit. Not saying anything is the best policy. Keeping your head down and doing what you're told is what we're expected to do. I wish I hadn't, though. I wish I knew what was really going on so I could have stopped it all.

"I think your uncle ..." I say and swallow thickly, knowing how this is going to sound and praying he'll believe me, "set it up. All of it."

"What do you mean 'all of it?'" His eyes narrow and Kat's gaze moves to her clasped hands on the table.

"Can we eat?" Kat pipes up between us, her nervousness not at all disguised by her sweet, feminine tone. I've always thought she was beautiful, but more than that, careful and intelligent. She has intention behind every move.

Cill peers down at her. "I'm not hungry." The way his eyes search hers is telling. He still loves her deeply, even if there's pain there.

I'm thankful for that. I would never forgive myself if he stopped loving her. How could he, though? The two of them need each other.

My throat is tight as I swallow and watch her tell him, "I think we should get some food first." Kat puts her hand over his. "I think we would all feel better if we had a bite to eat. A lot happened tonight."

While they share a hushed discussion and then call the waiter who silently brings silverware and menus, I think about how it got this bad. I remember every day that led to this hell.

The only thing worse than losing Cill and watching everything turn to shit, was figuring out that his uncle had been behind it all. For a while, I couldn't even admit it to myself. If I thought it was true, I'd have no choice but to tell Cill.

That would tear him up. When I finally decided it was real, a few months after his father passed, though I didn't have any proof, I found reasons not to tell him. If I told him while he was locked up, he'd go crazy. Cill could never sit around and let shit happen to him. He had to take action. At least he had to find out why something had happened, and maybe solve the problem. Going to him with vague rumors while he was in jail would cause havoc and put him in jeopardy.

I couldn't tell anyone. I did what we were told to do all our lives, keep our heads down and do what we were told.

All the while, I watched and caught on to the shit Eamon was doing and now I know too much.

When the waiter finally comes around, with a paper pad in his hand, I can barely find my words. It's like I've been slowly unraveling the last year, when all of this started after Cill's father died, and now there's nothing left of me.

As another waitress quietly comes into the room to refill Kat's goblet of ice water with the silver decanter—neither Cill or I have touched ours—our waiter asks what I'd like to order.

I peer across the table to ask what Kat and Cill ordered, a glass of red and two fingers of whiskey. Yeah, I'm probably going to need alcohol too.

Clearing my throat, I ask for the same as Cill. When the waiter's gone Kat speaks up again, her fingers slipping down the stem of her goblet.

"I think we each have one drink to calm our nerves, we eat to settle our stomachs and then we can talk," she states softly but in a matter-of-fact way, only lifting her gaze to reach each of ours once she's finished.

"We've spent hours in the car in silence, what's another hour here?" she points out as if it's an innocent question.

The tension still bristles from Cill's shoulders but he peers at me, waiting for my answer.

"Yeah," I reply, "I think that's best."

Turmoil stirs in the pit of my stomach as Kat orders us appetizers of bruschetta and burrata that sound far too eloquent for men like us, but the way she reads it and admits she loves the glaze has me nodding my head in agreement.

We all order meals. I go with the same meal I get every time we're here simply out of habit. Capellini with crabmeat. Cill and Kat do the same; filet and shrimp for Cill, and lasagna for Kat.

It's quiet while we wait, each of us thinking maybe. Taking small sips of my drink, I watch the two of them touch. Occasionally she holds his hand and he squeezes hers. It feels like an ending, like I'm forced to watch it, to sit in it so it's burned into my memory what real love is and how I almost destroyed it.

The whiskey is gone sooner than I'd like. I pick at the bread, not tasting it until the meals are served.

Kat was right. It's helping Cill, at least. He's not as tense. Kat watches him even more than I do.

I didn't know how things would go when we showed up on her front porch this past weekend. I was scared to death. If she kicked him out, I didn't think Cill was going to recover. She barely speaks to me anymore. She stopped talking to him too.

Now, staring across the table, I know everything happens for a reason.

It was one thing for him to lose his freedom for four years. It would have been another thing to have the one girl he loved most shut the door in his face.

Cill's plate is gone in minutes. I've barely touched mine and Kat's made a small dent in hers. But he inhales his dinner.

A faint smile tugs at my face when I remember the time we were here last and Cill was going off about something. She said he needed to eat and then he wouldn't care about whatever it was he was complaining about. I remember laughing but not paying attention to whether or not it was true back then. It's only a joke but I wish it were true. I wish a good meal and a conversation were all it would take to fix this.

Kat pushes the basket of bread in front of him. It's the best bread in the city. The inside is soft and the outside is crusty. It tastes like home. This restaurant is almost as familiar as the rec room at the garage. I know this bread like I know the recliners in that room. We must've spent hours there watching football and poker games.

Cill's eaten enough food for the three of us but it's done him some good. He might be different than he was before, but he's still my best friend. The hurt look in his eyes has faded a bit. Enough that we can talk.

The waitress brings dainty mugs of coffee once the waiter has cleared our plates. It's all done silently. Kat has tea instead. She stirs in sugar, the spoon clinking against the ceramic. I can feel her discomfort as well, though she's trying to hide it. For Cill's sake, I think. She glances over at me.

I take that as a signal to start talking.

"I think …" I start, then trail off and lick my lower lip, knowing what I'm about to say is a bombshell that could destroy Cill. But he has to know. "It wasn't just Kat's father who ratted four years ago."

Cill narrows his eyes, his brow pinching. His tone is level and low when he says, "The hell do you mean? Everybody knows it was him. He's the one who called Kat to warn her what was happening."

"And that didn't seem off to you?"

"No," answers Cill.

"It seemed off to me. The more I think about it, the more it doesn't make any sense." I look at Kat. "If your dad knew ahead of time, he wouldn't have let you go to Cavanaugh Crest that night. He didn't want you mixed up in all of that. He has his sins to pay for, but he loved you. It just doesn't fit."

Kat looks down at her empty plate. Cill's still looking at me, his eyes questioning.

"I don't think your dad died of a heart attack either," I tell him. I've held this knowledge for so damn long, and it's a relief to get it out into the open. "I think your uncle wants it all and he's working for both sides. The Ruin and the feds."

My mind races with a million things.

The fact that Missy went missing and his uncle claimed she was a rat and that she took off. Yet her house was cleaned out months later and she hadn't taken anything.

"I think he set her father up. I think Missy caught on and your uncle killed her. I think we have the cops come every other fucking month because he's slowly taking out anyone who stands in his way. I think it was supposed to be me that left when the cops came last."

"Slow the fuck down," Cill demands, his eyes locked on mine, his voice so low it's barely heard. Barely moving at all, he commands, "Start from the beginning."

With a racing heart, I swallow and tell him everything.

"When you left and her father disappeared, the charges they brought against you ... her father didn't know it all, you know? He didn't know about the frequency of drops ... it had to be someone else and Missy brought that up." I can barely breathe remembering how it all went down, but how Eamon played it like it happened differently.

"When she disappeared, he said it made sense because

she was asking questions and poking around. He said she had to be a rat.

"But the questions she was asking weren't something a rat would want to know. She was trying to figure out who else was in on it—"

"Missy was like a second mom to me," Cill says, his hand firmly wrapped around Kat's.

"I know. So did your father." His eyes whip back up to mine at the mention of his dad.

"He wasn't with it like he was before you went away. But he never believed Missy could do that to him. I think he caught on. I think he figured it out. 'Cause they said he died of a heart attack, but I heard them fighting before that, Cill. He and your uncle were going at it. Everyone who's questioned your uncle Eamon left shortly after. Either they died or they were a supposed rat who disappeared."

"Why didn't you tell me?"

"I didn't have proof until Kat's place got broken into." A heat breaks out across every inch of my skin as I look at Kat. "I didn't tell you, but I found two bricks of coke in your guest room. The same stock he had me moving during the bust. He knew Cill was getting out and he planted it and was going to wait for the perfect time." I look back to Cill.

"It had to be Eamon. He was the only one with a key to the stock. He planted it at Kat's place and I bet his plan was to take me down as I was moving it, and then to get you for possession, blaming it on me. Then we're both out of his way."

I don't even know if what I said makes sense to them. If they'll connect the dots like I did. "It sounds fucking crazy, but it's the only explanation."

My pulse races, praying they believe me. I almost add that he's why I let Kat go. Eamon is why when she broke down and told me she couldn't ever see me again, that's why I let her back away. If she stayed close, he could see her as a threat too.

I was still there for her. Still someone she trusted and I would be there any time she was in need, but at a distance.

I can't bring myself to speak about her, though. There's too much that's already been said.

"Say something, man," I plead after a long moment of silence. "I've felt like I'm going fucking crazy and paranoid for a year now. Ever since your pops died."

"You think my uncle sold out my father, his brother?" Cill's voice breaks when he adds, "You think my uncle killed him?"

There's a long moment of staring into my best friend's eyes, telling him something there's no way in hell he'd want to believe and having no evidence at all, only a gut feeling. "Yeah."

"No." He's quick to deny it, shaking his head. Kat, though, she stares back at me, realization clear in her gaze. "No, you're wrong." I hear the betrayal in his voice. I felt the same thing when I figured it out. The Cavanaugh MC wasn't about backstabbing bullshit and stealing power. It was about the bikes, and goddammit, the family. Founded by two first-generation brothers and their buddy Finn, something like this ... it's soul shattering.

"I know it's hard to believe, but–"

"They were supposed to have each other's backs." He stabs his finger on the table, emphasizing his point. Readjusting in his chair, he starts to say something and then stops.

And then he does it again, choosing his words carefully. "My uncle was supposed to be the example. He's supposed to take care of all of us. And now you're telling me he's turned? You're telling me he killed my father?"

"I think he—"

"That's one fucked-up thing to say if you don't know–"

"Yes. They fought and then your father died suddenly of what they said was a heart attack, but the autopsy didn't confirm that. Then Missy started poking around and she died. He lied, said she left but I know she's fucking dead. Everyone who goes against him disappears and I know it was him who broke into Kat's house. I know for a fact it was him.

"I don't have evidence of everything, but I know he planted evidence in her home."

"What did you do with it?"

"The coke? I dumped it."

"When did you start thinking he killed my father?"

"It was only a thought a year ago when he died, but then it made sense when Missy disappeared. I just ... I didn't want to believe it."

CHAPTER 13

CILLIAN

Every memory I have of my uncle flashes before my eyes as I watch Kat and Reed share a glance. The fear that lingered in his gaze turned to comfort the moment he saw she was worried.

I don't miss the way she speaks to him, with a tone and submissiveness I once thought she held only for me. And with the expectation that he'll make it all okay. That he'll fix it. That he'll keep her safe.

"My uncle ..." When I clear my throat the two of them stare back at me, and Kat's quick to place her hand in mine. I pull it under the table, squeezing it tight.

With a heavy breath, Reed looks between the two of us. I've never seen him look the way he does. I know four years changed us both, and neither of us for the better.

"It was just too much, too heavy … for it to be true."

"What you're saying …" I can't even finish a fucking sentence. Something deep inside of me is screaming that it makes sense. That ever since my father died and my uncle didn't even come in and see me, ever since then I knew.

Swallowing thickly I tell him, "Even if he's not a rat, even if he's not working both sides, if he killed my father, his only brother …" I leave the last part unsaid. I'll fucking kill him.

Reed's statement is spoken lowly, his eyes peering back with mourning. "I know."

It's silent for a long moment.

"Back in a minute," Reed says, getting up from his seat. He heads down the hall into the main restaurant and when he opens the door, the din of the other patrons slips into our private room for a small moment until it's quiet again.

Kat flips our hands so she's holding mine. "You okay, Cill?" Her soft voice is the only sound I've wanted to hear all this time.

"Lots of memories here," I say gruffly. It's true. I used to come here with my dad. We would sit in this same room and talk about whatever came to our minds. Usually it was something to do with Cavanaugh or school. I thought we'd be doing this until he was an old man, but he never got the chance.

Now Reed's saying it's our own family who killed him.

Anger scorches inside of me, rising up like a slow tide and exhaustion is the only thing keeping it down. If my uncle is behind all this, then I took the fall for nothing.

"I'm starting to doubt everything," I admit to her. The statement comes with a wave of sadness and regret.

Her gentle murmur makes me take it back though, "Everything?" she asks. Her wide hazel eyes beg me not to regret her and damn, if she ever thought I'd give her up or that I would take back anything between us, she's gravely mistaken.

With my fingers slipping under her chin, I whisper against her lips, "Not you, my little hellcat." With a soft kiss against her lips, I add, "Not us."

"What Reed just said is heavy and this place has to be difficult to be in," she tells me once I drop my hand from her chin. Nestling in next to me, she molds her side to mine, but stares at the door.

"Yeah, it's getting to me." I bite my tongue before saying the second half: *and I believe Reed*.

"You want to go home?" Kat murmurs.

"Not yet."

I want to sit here until I figure something out. I don't know what, exactly. Just something. I don't want to take this unsettled feeling back to her place with us.

The owner pokes his head in the door before coming out to see us. The sight of Nello makes my lips pull up in an asymmetric smirk. He's older than I remember him, with gray hair around his temples that was never there before and wrinkles around his eyes when he grins and says, "Cillian, how are you doing, young man? Is there anything I can get you?"

"No, thank you, Mr. Russo. I appreciate you letting us have this table last minute."

His hands clasp in front of him as he fiddles with his red tie. With black suit pants and a crisp white dress shirt, it's obvious he's the one in charge of this place. "Of course. It's the least I could do. I'm so sorry about your father," he adds, his tone somber.

Immediately, that bit of warmth I held vanishes. "Thank you."

He seems to regret his condolences, quickly turning his attention to Kat. "Is there anything I can get you, dear?"

Dear. He's forgotten her name. I know she hasn't been here as much as me, but she came with me a handful of times.

"No, thank you," answers Kat. She tries to put a smile on her face, but it's not real. Kat gives up halfway through. That scares the hell out of me. She always could do that. Smile when everything was going to shit.

With a nod, I think he'll leave us to it, but before he turns, he asks me, "You doing okay?"

"I'm glad to be out."

"You have everything you need?"

I've known this man for almost as long as I can remember. What Reed said has me questioning everything.

"Can I get you dessert?"

I didn't think I could eat another bite, but Kat perks up when she hears about dessert.

"Chocolate cake sound okay?" he asks her.

"Sure does. Maybe to go?" she adds and he says, *of course.* That's what he always says. He's amenable to men like me.

He glances down at our hands on the table as Reed comes back into the room. "What happened to your hand? You need anything for that?"

It's kind of him to ignore the matching bruises Reed and I are sporting. I flex it, stretching out my fingers and shaking my head as Reed takes his seat. "I tried to become a handyman and did something dumb with a hammer. Won't make that mistake again."

"Be more careful," he scolds, smiling with his eyes.

"Hey, Nello," I say before he can exit the room completely.

"What's that, Cill?"

"If anybody asks, we were here a little earlier. In fact, we've been back here all day."

He nods shortly, his gaze staying on mine. "You got it."

The moment the door closes, giving us privacy once again, Reed speaks, "Well, you didn't kill me. So I take it, what I said about what happened and about your uncle–"

Readjusting in my seat, I cut him off. "We'll talk about it later," I tell him and then glance between the two of them. "I want to," I start but shut my mouth as the waiter enters the room.

He brings chocolate cake packaged in a little black box tied with a red ribbon, halting the conversation.

I'm short with him, but my voice is as even as it can be. "Just the bill and a few more minutes, please."

"I want to talk about you two," I tell them both the moment the stiff silence greets us once again. "What the hell happened to you?" My gaze is solely on Kat.

She swallows thickly and pulls her hands into her lap. "What do you mean?"

"You're not yourself." I know it's hypocritical coming from me, but it's true. "You're scared and unsure and you," I say and bring my attention to Reed, motioning toward him, "you fucked Reed … was that before or after you ended it with me?" I didn't mean to say that last part. Fuck, I don't want to know. "I never thought you'd do that. What happened to my hellcat?"

"I—" Kat looks down at her chocolate cake, then back up at me. "I lost everything. I lost you … and then … I felt like I didn't deserve you."

Tears shine in her eyes and her face flushes. It kills me to see her this way. She isn't like she used to be. This strong woman who could handle anything. Hell, maybe it's me who remembers her differently … or maybe it's just because we were kids who didn't know shit.

I grab her hand again. "I love you, Kat."

Her eyes meet mine, disbelieving and filled with tears. "Cill ..."

"I love the woman you were," I tell her and make sure she's staring back at me when I continue, "and the woman you are now. Let me see you smile again. I want to make you smile again."

"I don't know if I can do that right now," she murmurs.

I let my mind unravel, every thought slipping out, "You weren't scared of anybody. You didn't cry yourself to sleep at night. You didn't refuse to smile. And you didn't fucking cheat on me."

Her eyes come to mine, glossy with tears. She doesn't deny it. That it happened before she ended it with me. *Fuck.* Dread pricks across my skin.

"Why?" I'm barely paying attention to Reed anymore. He hasn't said a word and I can't look away from Kat. "Why did you do it?" My throat's tight and dry.

She glances at the door. "We shouldn't have this conversation here. If you want to talk, we should go home."

"I'm not going home until you tell me why you thought it was better to cheat on me than wait just one more year." My pulse races. "You stayed through the hardest shit. Even when my father died ..." I'm losing my shit, and I know it. Emotions surge through me and make me want to punch something, or fuck something. It blew a hole through my chest to hear about her and Reed. I'm not going to spend another second sitting nicely at the dinner table while she keeps this secret from me. Hiding it does even more damage.

"I just don't think—"

"Why, Kat? Why did you do it? I was in prison, I lost my father." I can't help that my voice raises as I pound a fist to my chest. "I deserve an explanation."

Kat snaps, the fire coming back into her eyes. She digs her fingernails into the tablecloth. "You were angry," she says, her voice shaking with emotion. "Everyone hated me, and I lost them. I lost everyone."

"There's no way they hated you," I tell her, but I'm not sure. I don't know. I wasn't there, because I was in prison. I should have been by her side.

"Your father was the only one that still accepted me at Cavanaugh. He was there when my father left." Her voice tightens and she takes in a heavy breath before continuing. "And you were so angry and hateful and turning into someone I didn't recognize." Her voice drops. My hellcat is beautiful when she's pissed like this and all her angry energy is focused on me. Tears glisten on her cheeks but they're not a sign of weakness. It's like she's crying broken glass and doesn't care. "And I just wanted to be held for a moment. I wanted someone to say I wasn't crazy and that it was going to be okay, and you—you—"

She shakes her head, pulling back. The blaze in her eyes becomes less heated.

"You had too much, it was too heavy and I couldn't hold any more, Cill. We got into that fight–"

"It was one fight—" I argue back. I remember it well. I raised my voice at her. I vented. I took my anger out on her. I know I did. I apologized a hundred times, but I know I lost her that day. How could I have possibly kept her? I was fucking locked in a cage. I couldn't make it right.

"It wasn't just a fight. It was me realizing I couldn't help you anymore."

"So we got in one fight and you–"

"You're not listening," she says, cutting me off, her anger blistering between us. This ... this is what I know. The woman here I know how to handle.

"I needed you. I couldn't have you."

"So you went to Reed?"

"He came to me ... and I couldn't say no, because I needed someone to love me. I'm sorry"

"I never stopped loving you."

"It wasn't your fault. I'm not saying that." She's on edge, barely containing herself. "I'm sorry." She's at war with her anger and I've been here before with this woman. Only then she didn't hold back, she let me have it. Which is exactly what I deserved.

"Kat, I never stopped loving you."

"I love you, Cill. I've always loved you. I was just so lost and upset. And so damn alone."

"Come here."

I pull her into my lap and kiss her. I can taste her tears on her lips, but as soon as her mouth is on mine she's fully my hellcat again. I taste her like I haven't had the chance for four years. I kiss her like we might not have another chance when we walk out of here. Kat pulls back and I let out a sigh. It feels like I've been holding it in for my entire life.

"What was that?" she questions.

"My hellcat just came back to me." I put my hands on the small of her back and hold her closer. "Hit me."

"What?"

"Hit me, Kat." She puts her hands on my shoulders instead. "Curse me out. Do whatever you need to, but don't you dare leave me."

She laughs and wipes away her tears. "Where would I go, Cill?"

"Anywhere you wanted."

"It wouldn't matter," she tells me. "You're in my head, and in my heart. You'd still be with me. Except I wouldn't have you to talk to, and that would be hell. I know it would be, because it was hell when you went away."

"It was hell for both of us."

"You were fucking stupid to take the fall and say it was yours." There she is. That's my hellcat. I'm so damn relieved she's back. She would call me out back then, and I want her to do it now. "Possession and distribution. You should have kept your mouth shut and not said it was yours."

"I know. I was stupid. I thought I was doing a good thing. It didn't take long to realize I had fucked up."

"I hated you for it, Cill," Kat admits. She knows I can take it. That's what I wanted from her all along. I don't want her to treat me like I'm made of glass. "I hated that you did it and I watched you wither away." Her eyes shine with tears again. "I still loved you, even when I hated you."

"Well, I'm back, and I'm not going anywhere. I love you, Hellcat."

"I love you too."

She leans in and gives me a sweet, soft kiss. It reminds me of the way we used to kiss when we were teenagers and still figuring out how to do it right. Kat's always done it right. She can be a hellion, but she always kissed like we were in love.

I guess we were.

I know we still are.

Kat looks into my eyes, and I get lost in the moment. It's too damn much for the dinner table but I don't care. The only way I was going to walk out of here is if I solved something. Now we've solved it. And if there's still bullshit with Cavanaugh to be dealt with, at least we have an understanding of one another.

Her eyes go wide. "Oh no. Reed—"

We both turn to where Reed was sitting and find the chair empty.

CHAPTER 14

KAT

I'm exhausted when we get back to my house and the heartache is too much to deal with. The night has been far too long. "I just want to lie down," I tell Cill as I lock up behind us.

The keys hit the table and then I check my phone again. No reply from Reed. He left without a word, but Cill's car and keys were waiting for us in his place.

"On the couch, or in bed?"

"In bed." I need to be completely horizontal or I won't make it. Everything we talked about at the restaurant feels unfinished and painful. It's like a chilled dread that simply won't go away. Being on my feet one more second can't happen, though.

We both take quick turns in the bathroom and when I come out Cill is standing at my bedroom door. "I'm not sleeping anywhere else tonight."

That scares me, because it means he wants to keep talking too. And if we keep talking, I'm going to have to tell him all of the truth. There's a part I left out. A part that still hurts to talk about.

Yeah, he yelled at me because I was the only person there.

Yeah, he was stupid and then angry and there was nothing we could do about it.

Yeah, we were all dealing with the loss of his dad.

Yeah, without his dad there, I wasn't welcome at the club.

But there's a piece he's missing.

The bed welcomes me with its soft sheets and blankets I picked out with Lydia when I first moved in here. I burrow against the pillow while Cill climbs in next to me. He takes out his phone, and I see Reed's name on the screen. Text messages. Cill glances over them and puts the phone facedown on the table.

I move in closer to his side and let him put his arm around me. He reaches over and turns off the light.

With the room dark and quiet, I thought I'd be able to give in to the weight of the day and pass out. Instead my thoughts race and apparently so do Cillian's.

"Was it something specific I said that drove you away?"

Thump. My heart is heavy with every beat. "No ... I just

missed you and what we had before," I begin, and I know it sounds awful as soon as the words are out of my mouth. "I didn't mean that I was trying to replace you, or … or that you could be replaced. But I missed you. I was a wreck without you. I felt like there wasn't a reason to keep going. I'd wake up in the morning and think about going back to sleep for the entire day."

Cill rubs my back. "I thought about that too."

I roll over under the sheets and scoot closer to him, resting my cheek against his chest. He's quick to wrap an arm around me, holding me there. "There wasn't really anyone else who understood. Reed was the only other person who missed you like I did. Well, almost as much. I couldn't talk about it with anyone from Cavanaugh. I didn't even want to be back there. I would have been totally alone without Lydia and Reed, and Lydia didn't understand the way I was feeling."

He doesn't say anything. I know how this must sound. Me, complaining about how difficult things were for me when he was the one who truly suffered.

"I'm not comparing it," I murmur. "I know it was hell for you. You never should have gone away."

"It was worse than hell." Cill must have so many things bottled up inside, but he doesn't add anything else. I wait for a while to make sure.

"It was about missing you," I explain, hating how stupid it sounds. "It was about trying to live with that emptiness.

That's all it was."

His hand moves again on my back. "When did it happen?"

I wish I could just fall into the darkness with him and forget all of this ever happened. The sheets rustle as I maneuver under them, playing he won't push me away. Denying the past won't get rid of it. It won't change what I did with Reed. All it will do is force me to spend more energy pretending that my life played out differently. I don't want to do that.

"The first time was after your dad died." Reed and I had both gone to the funeral. I felt like my dress was choking me. The service was filled with people from Cavanaugh Crest and all I wanted to do was escape. I didn't want to keep the life I had. "The funeral was hard. Reed was devastated that you couldn't be with us. He said it was fucked up that you couldn't be there. He wouldn't drop it."

"How long after?"

"A few weeks." I steel myself to continue. "Then you stopped answering my calls and when I went in, we had that fight."

Anger spills out of him. "So you thought it would be better to fuck my best friend?" I begin to pull away, but Cill holds me tight. "Kat—I'm sorry. Fuck."

"I know. I know. I'm sorry."

"It already happened," Cill says. I get the impression he's repeated this to himself many times over the past four years. "It's done. It hurts like hell, but it's done."

The words are right there, wanting to be heard, but he continues instead, "Not being able to see you was the lowest moment in my life. And then you stopped coming altogether."

I can feel him hesitating over a question.

"Just ask," I plead. This is so damn painful. It's the hardest conversation I've ever had because I need us to come out better after this. I can't lose him again. Cill's the only reason I'm not crying already. I sure as hell want to. The tears are nearly ready to flow. The guilt churns in my stomach.

Far off in the distance, almost so far we can't hear it, a police siren disturbs the city.

"And you still have feelings for him?" Cill asks although it's not so much a question, just a known truth.

I don't lie to him. "Yeah ... I still have feelings."

"Did he wear a condom?" Cill asks.

I knew he would say that, but my stomach drops. "No."

"You could have gotten pregnant."

My teeth lock together like they don't want to let out the words. I don't want to give voice to the words. Every day I've tried to come to terms with this. To accept it as something I did that's not any better or any worse than anyone else's actions. But it is worse, because it was Reed. Because Cill had lost his freedom. I still had mine, and I used it to royally fuck up.

I can't speak. The longer my hesitation lasts, the surer he's going to be.

"You told me not to hold back," Cill says gruffly. "Now

you don't hold back."

"I did." There. He knows now. I said it, and he knows. "I did get pregnant."

As he props himself up to stare down at me, I fall to the sheets, the tears flowing, but nothing else does. "Hellcat ..."

I've made it this far without breaking down. That won't last forever.

"I found out two months in when I miscarried."

Cill sucks in a breath. The shadows that line his face highlight the pain in his expression. I swear I see him wipe under his eyes just as I look at him, but I can't be entirely sure because he leans down to kiss the crook of my neck the moment I think he's crying.

I made a mistake and I suffered it alone.

Besides watching Cill get arrested, the miscarriage was the worst experience of my life. At first I didn't know what was happening. I hadn't been paying much attention to my cycle because I couldn't bring myself to care about anything. Everyone knows that stress can cause you to be late. That's what I thought, if I thought about it at all.

Then the bleeding started. The pain was what made me realize it wasn't normal. I was only eight weeks along but it hurt so badly I couldn't stand up. Every time I tried, I'd get dizzy. I thought I might die in my own bathroom.

Nobody else was there.

I wasn't talking to Reed after what happened. It was

awful what we'd done.

Cill wasn't talking to me either. We had the fight and then I went silent and he gave me the silent treatment back.

So when I realized … all I thought was that I deserved to go through that pain alone.

Lydia was at work with her phone off.

I caved and called the only person who could take me to the hospital, but Reed wasn't answering. And the person who I wanted to hold me and promise me it would be okay was locked in a prison cell.

That pain hits me all over again and I push Cill's arm off me and try to stand up. Cill won't let me leave. He pulls me back into the bed with him.

"I have to go," I say, my voice thick with tears and shove my hand against him. "I don't want to do this in front of you."

His strong arms wrap around me and pull me close to him, bringing me into a comforting warmth.

With his lips brushing a kiss in the crook of my neck, he whispers, "That's not true and you know it." Without an ounce of fight in me, I give in, letting him pull my body as close to his as possible as he runs his hand over my hair. "You missed me like I missed you, Hellcat. Don't try to lie to me about it."

"Why should you watch me cry over this? It was my mistake. I deserve to work through the consequences on my own. You shouldn't feel sympathy for me, Cill. I knew it was wrong and I did it anyway."

"Yeah. You were hurting and you tried to seek out comfort. You think I can blame you for that? I did the same damn thing, only there was nowhere to go but inside my head. I'm partly to blame for all this shit happening anyway."

"No you're not."

"I could have seen you sooner," he admits. "After the fight. I thought if I put you out of my mind, the time would pass quicker. It was bullshit. And by the time I got over it, you had stopped coming."

"I felt too guilty to come. I couldn't look you in the eye knowing what I'd done."

"I'll look you in the eye any time," he says, and I finally let myself melt into his arms.

"Will you be able to do it in the morning?" I question. I don't know if I'd be able to, if I were him. I might get up and walk out like he did that first night he stayed.

"I'd look at you any damn morning, Hellcat. I don't care what happened."

"Yes you do, Cill."

"I care. But I only care because it's you. I want you to be okay."

Deep, even breaths are all I'm able to focus on and the warmth of his chest against my back. I listen to his heartbeat for a while. A long while maybe, his arm a comforting weight around me, holding me close and refusing to let go. His breathing steadies long before mine does.

"That's it," I tell him. "I didn't do anything else while you were gone. I hope you can believe me when I say that."

"Hmm?" Cill asks sleepily. I blink up at his face. It's mostly hidden in the dark, but I'm pretty sure his eyes are closed.

"I'm glad you came back," I whisper, and then I curl up against him and fall asleep too. "I love you, Cillian."

CHAPTER 15

KAT

Cillian and Reed sit close together at a new kitchen table Reed brought over this morning and the two of them put together in silence while I slept. Cill's still in his gray sweatpants and a white tee. Reed's at least dressed in jeans and a dark navy Henley.

With sleep still in my eyes, I came down to see the two of them putting the last screws in. Reed can barely look me in the eye and the only thing he's said to me is that he's sorry he didn't answer last night. He had a lot to think about.

There's a sadness between us that doesn't fit right but I've tried to swallow it down all morning.

I made them coffee an hour ago and I know for a fact it's cold by now. Neither one of them seems to have noticed.

They just keep talking in low voices that make it impossible to hear a damn thing.

I should be grateful that they're both there, sitting side by side, not murdering each other.

"More coffee?" I ask, holding up the pot. I've had two cups and it's still not enough to make me feel awake enough for whatever's going on.

They don't answer. I pick up the two mugs. They don't notice. I dump them out in the sink. Still nothing.

"Are you going to let me in on what you're planning? I know it has to do with Cavanaugh." I fill up the mugs with fresh coffee and take them back to the table.

"I don't think this is something you need to be a part of, Kat," Reed says, accepting his coffee and still not looking me in the eye. I fucking hate it.

Blowing out my frustration, I close the cabinet door carelessly after putting the sugar back and say, "Cillian, if you're going back to the Crest to deal with your uncle, I deserve to know about it."

"When it's all said and done, Hellcat," Cill answers, blowing across the top of his coffee. He doesn't look me in the eye either.

I bang my fist on the table between them. It finally makes Reed shut up. "Tell me," I demand. "I don't know what the hell you two think you're doing. You didn't tell me shit back then, but you're going to tell me everything right now or I'll fucking lose it, Cill. You too, Reed. What the hell is going on?"

Cill's lips pick up in a smirk. "Well good morning, Hellcat," he murmurs, his pale blue eyes piercing right through me in a way that's sinful.

I'm caught for a moment as he sips his coffee.

"I thought you could hear us, Hellcat."

"How could I possibly hear you when you're whispering?" I bend down and kiss his cheek, leaving both palms on the table and leaning down low enough that I'm more than sure he can see right down my baggy sleep shirt. "Tell me. Now."

Reed and Cill share a glance that would piss me off if I wasn't sure I had their attention. "We're figuring out what to do with him," Reed says.

"Who?"

"My uncle," Cill says. Pain flashes in his eyes as fear engulfs me. "We're comparing notes. Figuring out what really happened."

Reed stands up from his seat before Cill is finished speaking. "I've got to go call someone. I'll be back in a minute."

"Where are you going?" I ask.

"Just to the porch," he answers and knowing he's not going far settles the unease inside of me.

"Don't do anything stupid," I tell him although I'm not sure he hears as the front door shuts, my throat thick with frustration. This was how they were before Cill went away.

Planning things together. Getting in trouble together. I could talk them out of things, but honestly, I didn't most of the time. I was always riding in the passenger seat and chiming in to tell the stories later at Cavanaugh. Nothing major. We never got arrested. But I was Cill's hellcat, for better or for worse.

I'm older now, though, and someone has to think about these things.

"What exactly are you two going to do?" I say and glare at Cill. An amused smile curves his lips and he stands up from his seat at the table. My heart pounds like they're taking action right this minute instead of just making plans.

"Don't be scared, Hellcat."

"I'm not scared." The words stumble off my lips as I make my way back to the corner of the cabinets, leaning against the counter. "I'm pissed. I'm fucking pissed, Cillian." I take refuge in my mug of coffee.

He crosses the kitchen, the legs of the chair scraping across the linoleum floor as he gets up.

"You don't look pissed," he counters, his steps steadily bringing him closer to me. The mug clinks on the counter as I set it down, my attention never leaving Cill. "Fine ... maybe I'm scared."

He closes the distance between us and rests his forehead against mine before kissing the tip of my nose and whispering, "Yeah. Me too."

As much as I love his comforting touch, I pull away, making sure he understands how serious I am.

"I'm scared to lose you—I can't go through that again." His lips brush against mine in an attempt to silence me, calm me, or just love on me, I'm not sure. But I can't shake this uncertainty so I gently push him back. "If your uncle planted shit here when he broke in—if he's already trying to fuck you over—I'll fucking kill him." The words leave me without a second thought. Peering up at Cillian, I watch his brow raise and then the grin grow on his handsome face, his cheek still bruised.

"My little hellcat," Cillian says, and he kisses me. Not just a light peck. It's not a move to soothe me. It's a kiss I know he needs just as much as I do.

And just like then, his mouth on mine makes me forget to fight everyone.

It makes me forget we're up against his uncle, and seemingly the rest of the world. He flicks his tongue against mine and I forget it all. I forget to be heartbroken that Cavanaugh let me down after Cill's arrest. I forget everything but how good it feels to be with him.

The hum of the refrigerator kicks on and I fall deeper into the kiss.

Cill pushes me up against the counter, the space between us lighting on fire. As he presses up against me, I'm made aware that Cill's hard and I tease myself by rubbing against him until he groans. "If you're going to do that, Hellcat, we should find a bedroom."

Just then Reed comes back in, the front door slamming shut behind him. "Damn it," Cill says. He kisses me one more time and pulls away.

Reed's footsteps are heavy and I'm still catching my breath as Cill turns to face him. It doesn't make sense that I should feel as guilty as I do when Reed catches my eye.

"What did he say?"

"Yeah. He meets every other week." He paces through the kitchen, his hand running through his hair. Cill glances back at me as I ask, "What's going on?"

"My uncle was seen with a man a few times. Reed hired someone to follow him after he found the coke upstairs. He's an agent."

"An agent? Like–"

"Like, an agent of the Federal Bureau of Investigation … my uncle's the rat."

Reed chimes in. "If he's working for the feds, what the fuck are we going to do?"

"I'm not leaving," Cill says.

Reed stares at him. "Why the fuck would you stay? I've wanted out since you left. It's been fucking hell."

"You think there's nothing worth fighting for? What about Finn?"

"He thinks the same," Reed counters. "He's counting the

fucking days. He told me when you got out—someone was going to die. I can feel it, Cillian."

Cillian's silence speaks to his disagreement.

"You don't know how far it's gone." Reed is quiet and serious.

"Nobody else is going to jail because of him. If someone's going down, it's going to be my uncle."

"Then I hope it's only him that's a rat. 'Cause if it's anyone else, we're fucked."

My stomach knots as my mind speeds ahead through what that would mean.

If Cill's uncle has gotten his claws into Cavanaugh, they're already against us. If more of them are working with the feds, then it means there's no safe place for Cill to be anymore. Just avoiding the club won't be enough. They'll be looking for ways to put him back in jail.

But more than that, it'll mean that the family we once had is as good as dead.

"It's worth it," Cill says. "If there's a chance to put it back together again, we have to take it."

"It's not fucking worth it," Reed argues. "Do you hear what you're saying? It's not worth it for you to be in jail!" Reed's voice breaks on the last word. Everything he feels echoes in myself.

"Cillian, please—" I start to say, trying to reason with him.

"If my uncle comes after us, that's just as bad as being

locked up. Fuck it, Reed. I'm not going to spend the rest of my life looking over my shoulder. If you really think he's all there is to Cavanaugh, then by all means, don't try to take him down. But I think you know better."

"Damn it, Cill." Reed shakes his head.

Cill looks at me. "What do you think, Hellcat? You think it's over at Cavanaugh?"

All of my earliest memories of the club flick through my mind. I was at home in the rec room, and the garage. I never felt out of place there. Even as a little girl, if I wanted to know something about one of the bikes, some tall man wearing black leather and a grin would explain it to me.

Cavanaugh's the reason we're all standing in this kitchen together. If we hadn't had that, we wouldn't be here.

And Cavanaugh's been dead to me since Cill's father was buried six feet under.

"If your uncle's working with the feds, I think you tell the Cross brothers, you tell the Valettis. You let it leak to the men who can take care of it and we get the hell out. Ask someone at The Ruin where we can go."

"Where's my hellcat?" Cill murmurs, disappointment evident.

"Protecting you, Cillian. Keeping you from getting in deeper when you never should have been involved."

"Listen to her, please, man," Reed pleads with Cillian who looks between the two of us with disbelief.

"It's the Crest ... what are you two fucking saying—"

"The Crest is dead!" Reed screams, desperate to get through to Cill. He closes the space between them with heavy steps and the air suffocates me. "The club is down to ten people including the two of us. Six men I hardly know anymore, a traitor and an old man who's waiting to die." I reach out to steady Reed, slipping between the two of them as the tension rises. He's losing it.

"Hey, hey, let's just have a seat," I offer, gentling my touch. I've only seen Reed like this once before. The day Cillian's dad was found dead. My hands rest against his shoulders and Reed's arm wraps around my waist, pulling me in as he buries his head in the crook of my neck.

I'm surprised but only because Cill's behind us.

"I can't do it," Reed murmurs before coming to grips and slowly releasing me. He lifts his head, his eyes red and drops his trembling hand. "I can't watch you kill yourself for a family that doesn't exist anymore."

Everything in me wants to hold on to him as he takes a step backward.

He stares at Cillian and I'm hesitant to look back and see his expression. I expect anger from Reed holding onto me like that. Maybe even toward myself for getting between them. I expect a lot of things, but when I turn around, Cill is right there, reaching around to pull Reed in. I'm caught there, between them both, as Cill pats Reed's back with firm slaps.

"I'm right here, brother."

"Don't fucking go back, man. Don't fucking leave us again."

As I slip away from their embrace, the two men hug it out, neither willing to let go. "We have each other," Reed says and emphasizes, "that's enough."

Cillian's silent and I'm not certain he's convinced.

"Can we just wait to do anything?" I offer again. "We have time, don't we?"

The two men look over at me before they each take a step back, emotion riddled in their lost expressions. My two broken and lost men. "We have each other, that's what matters," I tell them.

Cillian looks between the two of us, swallowing thickly. "How exactly is that?" he questions and a chill sweeps down my back.

"What do you mean?" Reed questions in a single breath even though both of us know what he means. There's love between us all, and I can't deny that I feel more love for Reed than I should.

"I mean ... the two of you ... If I wasn't here, you'd be with her, wouldn't you?"

"No, the club isn't safe–"

"If it was safe," Cill says and inside I'm screaming for Reed to let it go. I love him, but he knows I'll always be Cill's. I can't lose him as a friend, though. Neither can Cill. We need each other. It's as simple as that.

Instead, he says the worst thing he could.

"Yeah." He swallows, his hands slipping into his pockets, as if signaling he doesn't want to fight, or maybe that he's willing to take the punch without punching back. "If you weren't here and it was safe, I'd be with her. Of course I would."

Thump, my heart races and a heat engulfs me.

"And you would too," Cill states softly, without judgment as he glances at me.

"But you are here," I say and the words are pleading as they pour out. I can't lose him. Please, no.

"I know I am, Hellcat. I'm not going anywhere," he tells me as I rush into him, my hands fisting his tee. He chuckles. The bastard chuckles a genuine laugh as he looks down at me, smoothing over my hair before kissing my temple.

I've never felt such confusion.

"The thing is," he whispers at my temple, his warm breath slipping down my shoulder, "Reed still wants to fuck you and you want him too." He keeps me close to him and before I can object, Reed agrees.

As I turn to face him, breathless, Reed is standing closer than before, only inches behind me now. "I never stopped wanting you and I never will, Kat."

Cill kisses the side of my neck, stealing my attention back. "What do you say, Hellcat? You want to be shared?"

CILLIAN

Kat keeps looking back at me like this can't be real. Every time her wide hazel eyes search mine, I kiss her harder, wanting that look of uncertainty to vanish.

The moment the three of us are inside her bedroom, I kick the door shut and tell her to strip. I'm the first to make a move, pulling my shirt over my shoulders and letting it fall to the floor.

Kat stares back but I don't have to ask her twice.

Her sleep shirt falls to the floor easily enough and she shimmies her thin lace panties down to the floor. Leaving her completely bared to us, her rosebud nipples peaked and her hair cascading around her shoulders.

Her wide eyes dart between the two of us, her shoulders rising and falling with each heavy breath. The flush in her cheeks and her hardened nipples prove she's turned on, even if nervousness clings to her.

"How do you want me?"

"On your knees, Hellcat."

I help her get into position exactly how I want her. On the edge of the bed, her mouth facing Reed who's still standing there, his shirt removed but his pants still on. I'm the first to drop my pants, palming my cock and stroking it once.

The bed groans as I climb up behind her. I'm vaguely aware that Reed has hardly moved. If he wants her, if wants to keep loving her like I know he does, this is the only way he's going to get her.

"You taking her pussy?" he finally asks lowly, just above a breath.

I only nod, knowing damn well I want her coming on my cock and I'll be coming inside of her. I get her first. She's mine, after all. I'm only sharing.

He crouches down and runs the pad of his thumb across her bottom lip as he asks, "You want me in your ass then, my little sex kitten?"

Her body tenses slightly and I run a soothing hand down her curves. "You did that?" I ask them both, purely out of curiosity.

Kat's head shakes and Reed says, *not yet*.

My cock hardens even more at his statement: not yet. There's so much pleasure we could show her together. So many things we've never done.

Excitement runs through me, but I focus on playing with her, on readying her.

"How about your mouth then?" Reed murmurs, leaning down to kiss her and she moans into the kiss. My heart races watching them.

It's not what I expected. There's no jealousy, only a need for more.

I press the head of my cock between her folds and then lower, spreading my precum around her clit.

She gives me a sweet little mewl and I focus on her rather than Reed, who's only watching so far.

Leaning down so my chest is closer to her and I can nip the lobe of her ear, I push my fingers inside of her, stroking and then pulling out to rub ruthless circles against her clit.

"You're so fucking wet, Kat." I nip her shoulder as I pull back and add, "Are you wet for him too?"

She doesn't answer at first, although I know she heard and I spank her ass, once. The slap reverberates in the room.

At first she cries out, but she's quick to answer, "Yes."

"That's my good girl." Reed says the words that were just about to come from me.

I settle on the next step as he gets into the position he wants, finally playing along.

"Arch your back how I like," I say and I watch as her ass raises and her shoulders drop.

"Keep that mouth of yours available for Reed while I fuck you," I tell her and just as she's answering, I slam deep inside of her in a single thrust.

Her gasp is fucking everything. I fuck her ruthlessly, thrusting into her at a deep and steady pace. Her nails dig into the comforter and she struggles to keep her head up as the pleasure tenses her body.

A part of me wants him to see what I do to her, how she's perfect for me. How easily I get her off and how gorgeous it is when she comes for me. The other part of me, a very curious part of me, wants to know if Reed can satisfy her too. I want to know if she makes those same sounds for him.

Licking his lower lip, Reed unzips his pants and lets them fall to the floor. Palming his dick, he watches me as I grip her shoulder, pounding into her mercilessly as she moans and struggles not to writhe under me.

Watching him hold her like that, her gaze pinned on his with his hand wrapped around her throat, is addictive in a way I've never felt. "You want me to throat fuck you while Cillian comes inside your tight little pussy?"

Wrapping her hair around my wrist, I fist the hair at the base of her neck and hold her steady for him.

"Open up that sweet mouth of yours," I command her and she obeys.

Her pussy tightens around my cock as I thrust myself as deep as I can inside of her.

She moans around the head of Reed's cock, her cheeks hollowing as he pushes himself in her.

His left hand stays around her throat as his right moves lower, so he can cup her breast in his hand. He plays with her, teasing her and I crave more of it.

His hips thrust and I watch as she tries to take him. My little hellcat takes what she can, her eyes watering and when she swallows around him, I nearly lose it.

Reed's head falls back and at the same time, she tightens around me. She loves it. The desire and the primal need that tenses every muscle in me are unimaginably sinful.

I fuck her harder as he pulls out and she heaves in a breath.

Her lips are swollen as he palms his cock, strokes it and then lifts her head back up. "You can take more of me," he tells her and she obeys, opening her mouth into that perfect O even as she moans from the hard thrusts I give her.

Fuck. I find my release, pulling out as quickly as I can and only exhaling as I come on her back.

"Take her pussy," I tell him, barely getting out the words as I heave myself up. With a hand on Kat's hip, I turn her over. It's careless, and we'll need to change the sheets once he's done, but I want to see him fucking her.

Selfishly, I want to be the first to throat fuck her.

"Spread your legs for Reed," I tell her and my little hellcat obeys, her pink pussy already swollen. Reed doesn't hesitate to climb on the bed as I get off. Breathing heavily and trying to wrap my head around how fucking hot this is.

If a man laid a hand on Kat or looked at her twice, I'd kill him. But Reed giving her pleasure like this? It's something I didn't know I'd enjoy like this.

Bringing her knees up, he pushes himself inside of her, and her head falls back, her eyes close and he thrusts as if he's meant to be fucking her. As if this is how he did it before. There's comfort in the position, his groin pressed against her clit, like he's all too aware that's how she likes it.

I wait for the jealousy, I wait for the anger, but all I can do is watch as he rocks inside of her and Kat opens her eyes to stare at me. Her eyes are wide until they close again, the pleasure taking over.

Reed chuckles a deep rough sound before kissing her neck, and it snaps me out of it. "Look at Cillian," he commands Kat, who's barely with it. "He's giving me a smug look, like your pussy only feels this good because he warmed you up for me."

Kat's bottom lip drops as she peers back at me, lust covering her gaze. With every thrust, she lets out a moan.

I wish I was hard again. I wish I hadn't come at all. I'm already planning on how I want to fuck her with Reed again. Next time I'll take her mouth first. And that sweet ass of hers is going to need to be prepped.

A low groan of approval leaves me and I crouch down to be closer to Kat.

"Be a good girl and please us both," I whisper as I kiss her. Her hazel eyes are half lidded as she moans my name. Mine, not his.

"I'm not the one fucking you right now, Kat." Reed lifts her knee up, slamming into her deeper and harder. "Come on his dick like you did for me."

It doesn't take long for them to each find their release and all the while I wait for the anger, for anything other than a deeply satisfied content.

Even when he comes in her, I fucking love it.

Even as her hand slips between her legs to keep from making even more of a mess, all I want is to replay what just happened over again.

It's quiet as he leaves her, gathering a hand towel from the bathroom and bringing it back to her.

She doesn't look at me and he doesn't either, not for a long time. Not until I help Kat up and the vulnerability stares back at me.

I kiss her. At first it's quick and then she reaches up for more and I mold my lips to hers.

"You able to stand, Hellcat?" I nip her lower lip as she straightens herself. "Barely," she manages and then blushes as she peeks up at me.

She's utterly gorgeous, with her hair a messy halo and her cheeks flushed. "I just need the bathroom." With a smirk on my lips, I help her get to the door. All the while Reed's in the background, taking off the sheets and laying down the comforter so we can sleep on that tonight.

Leaving her in the bathroom, I make my way back.

The moment we're alone, Reed questions, "So, you're not going to kill me then?"

"Is that what you thought?"

"For a moment ... I questioned it."

"Figured you'd try to get laid one more time before I ended you then?" I joke but he doesn't laugh.

"I mean it. I love her but I love you too. I just ... I don't want to lose either of you. I barely made it this last year."

It takes every bit of the man I am to admit to him the truth I had to accept last night, "I don't think I can keep her on my own. Not when I know she loves you like you love her."

"You could. She loves you more."

"Who would I be without you, though? I need you and if you're going to be here, you're going to be around her." I lick my lower lip, cutting him off when he takes pity on me, rather than simply accepting it.

"It's always been the three of us. I want to keep it that way and if it means, I share her ... then that's what it means."

I'd rather share her than lose her. Right now she might choose me, but when I fuck up again, and I know I will, I don't want her to question it. I want her to have my best friend right there, so she can confide in him and love on him until she's not angry at me anymore.

"I might lose her if it's only me, but together we can have her forever."

"You're talking like this is more than just a one-time thing," he states although it's more a question.

"It's whatever we want it to be. I want to take care of my uncle and get the hell out of here, maybe disappear to the West Coast?" Ever since Kat said the club was dead, it's slowly sunk in. Maybe I just needed to hear her say it, or maybe I needed the fear of losing her to settle deep into my bones. "All I know is that I lost you and her once, I'll do whatever we need to do, but I want to deal with my uncle before we head out."

Reed only stares back at me, nodding before telling me, "I'll see what I can find out."

CHAPTER 16

REED

It's late at night when I get the message from my guy at The Ruin. He knows somebody on the West Coast—a guy named Derrick who used to be tight with someone named Seth, the right-hand man of one of the Cross brothers. We were given the blessing to leave, to take refuge there with new IDs, new passports, a new life.

It's a gift in exchange for the information about Cillian's uncle Eamon. The Ruin verified it and said they'd take care of him, and it would be the end of the Cavanaugh Crest.

They didn't say we couldn't kill him first, though.

"Promise me you two won't do anything stupid." Kat's words ricochet in my head as the engine revs beneath me. She's made me make that promise a thousand times. I ride

behind Cillian in the dark of the night on the way to the Cavanaugh Crest, gripping the handlebar as the vibrations travel up, warning me that keeping that promise is going to take a fucking miracle.

We don't find Cill's uncle at the club. That would be an amateur move. I used my contact at The Ruin to set up a meeting at a place outside the city limits. There's a large reservoir there, and once something comes in, it doesn't come back out.

Still risky as hell to do this. We have no guarantees that someone else won't show up.

Hell, I'm relying on my contact from The Ruin to get Eamon here. I half expect Finn to be with him or serving as his lookout, although I was assured he'd come alone.

We park down the hill from the reservoir, side by side on our bikes and kill the lights. Fear and doubt creep in as we wait. "We could keep riding," I suggest to Cill. "We could pick up Kat and get the hell out of town."

I don't want her mixed up in this. It broke her heart when Cill went to prison. It doesn't need to happen twice. We can figure things out on the road.

Just us, getting the hell away. Ever since he suggested it, I can't stop thinking about it. It's the only thing that feels right anymore.

"If he killed my father ... you know he did. I know he did. I'm not leaving here till he admits it." With a nod, I follow him down to the meet. It's a hill between two old warehouses, the moonlight and security lights are all that help us see.

There's a good chance Cill's uncle doesn't show, either. There's a chance all of this is another setup.

We wait about five minutes and a light appears at the bottom of the hill. An old man, a touch overweight in dark jeans and a black hoodie, checking a cell phone. It's Cill's uncle.

"Holy shit," Cill says under his breath. "There he fucking is." My pulse spikes.

Although we see him, it takes him about halfway to realize it's us. He stops in his tracks as it registers. I wonder if he knows then. All I can think is he has to realize at some point tonight that we know. "Hey, Eamon," I call out, keeping my voice even and trying not to raise suspicion as his hand falls to his waistband. I can't come back alone. The thought is buried deep in the back of my mind.

The crickets and the night sounds surround us until all I can hear is my blood rushing in my ears. Eamon's eyes narrow. "You're not who I'm supposed to be meeting with."

"We got a message too." I keep my tone even. I don't want to scare him off. "It said to meet here and ask about Missy ... is that what you're doing here? Something about a rat?"

He laughs, nervousness filtering into it and I know he hears it just like the two of us do. Clearing his throat he adds, "Now they didn't tell me that. That's," he shakes his head, one hand running down his jaw, the other lingering over the gun tucked in his jeans.

"That's what?" Cill questions. "You sure she was a rat? We heard it might be someone else. We heard it might be you."

A moment of silence hangs over the hill.

"It's a shame," Cill's uncle says.

"What's a shame?" Cill asks.

"That it has to end this way," his uncle replies.

He pulls out the gun, recklessly in an attempt to be fast. I'm faster, though, prepared and aiming it at his skull without stumbling. His is still aimed at the ground, his hoodie having slowed him down.

"Lift it and I pull the trigger, Eamon," I tell him, my tone deadly.

"How about you drop it?" Cill says, the heavy gun in his hand slowly rising to aim at his uncle. "Tell us what happened. Did you kill my father?" A faint click tells me Cill's a hairline pull of a trigger from ending it all. A cold sweat breaks out across my skin.

Eamon's gaze goes from me to Cill. Gun or not, he's still outnumbered. He's going to have to hit us both if he wants to walk away from this place. There's no way that's happening. He swallows loudly and then gives a half-hearted smirk.

"Don't you boys think this is all a bit overblown?" he says, the breeze in the chill of the night carrying his voice to us. "This is a misunderstanding. Put down the fucking gun, Reed."

"A misunderstanding?" Cill says it slowly, like he can't

believe his uncle just said this to him. "Did you call my dad's death a misunderstanding?"

"That was a heart attack," his uncle snaps.

"That's not what I've heard," Cill says. "I heard different. I heard it was you." Emotion carries into his words. The mourning, the betrayal. "Are you gonna deny it?"

He waits and the silence stretches.

"You'd have done the same thing," spits his uncle. "Your father ran the club into the ground when you left. He refused to take the opportunities we were given ... so I took one instead."

Cill takes an uneasy step forward, a step too close for my liking. "You decided to get in bed with the feds and pick people off."

"At least I didn't get in bed with your old lady, like Reed did," Eamon shoots back. Cill's jaw clenches and for a second I'm worried he'll lose his temper, but he ignores the taunt.

"You set me up ... set Reed up?" He motions toward me with the gun and glances at me. His uncle doesn't, though, and I keep my focus on Eamon.

Bitterness seeps into Eamon's tone. "I did what I had to do."

"What the fuck?" Cill almost laughs. "Admit it. Admit you killed him."

Two things happen at once: Eamon lifts his gun and fires at the same time I pull the trigger. Cill's too lost in his emotions to act quickly enough, but I saw it. I saw Eamon's thumb move back. I pulled it as quickly as I could, but still, his uncle got off a shot.

Bang. Bang.

Heat overwhelms me and I'm paralyzed as I watch both of them drop. Eamon falls backward, a bullet ripping through his throat. Blood sprays and I take two steps forward, watching his hands attempt to keep the blood from gushing out of his neck, even as he chokes on it.

Training keeps me focused on him, even though fear cripples me. "Cill." I call out his name as the life drains from Eamon's body.

"Cill!" I call out louder as Eamon's eyes fall back and his body stills, his hand drops to the ground. His chest is still. I don't trust it. I move forward once more, aim the gun and shoot two more bullets into his chest. They thud one after the other, jostling his body from the force. There's no sound, no expression.

He's dead.

It's only then that I can move, turning to find Cill propped up on his knee. Thank fuck. Relief floods through me but I can't stop my hands from trembling.

"I thought you were dead." Adrenaline rushes through my veins. "I thought he got you."

"I'm all right," he tells me, although he stays focused on Eamon. "He didn't say it."

"I'm sorry, Cill." I know he wanted to hear it, he needed to. Fuck, I did too. I settle on a single truth. "He's a coward."

It takes two of us two drag him to the edge of the reservoir. We weigh down his pockets with rocks and throw him in. Doesn't take long for him to disappear under the water. Even after it's done, it doesn't feel real. None of it does. Not until Cill tells me, "Let's get home to Kat."

I only nod, keeping my answer to myself, but he says it. He says the exact words I was thinking, "I need her."

Kat

Cill and Reed thought they could tiptoe out of my house without me knowing, but they were wrong. I heard them leave.

I swear there's some part of me that just knows when they're in trouble. Like my soul is attached to theirs. And right now, it's worried.

I tried to fall back to sleep, it's what Cill would want. Instead I either stared at the spinning fan, thinking the worst, or tossed and turned … also thinking the worst.

They're gone long enough that after an hour of uselessness, I get out of bed and make a hot cup of tea.

It feels better to wait in the kitchen. Lying under the covers and hiding has never been my thing. Maybe for a couple of days after Cill got arrested, but you can't hide under the damn blankets forever. Eventually, the world finds you anyway.

Time slips by and I text Lydia. Her response is to call and the moment I answer she asks, "Want me to come over?"

"No, that's okay. I'm just–"

"Waiting for two men who are nothing but trouble," she half jokes, sleep evident in her voice.

"I didn't mean to wake you."

"I wasn't dreaming of anything special so I don't mind," she tells me. A sad smile graces my lips as I sit down at the table.

"How are you two?"

I chew my bottom lip at the word *two*. "We're ... kind of like old times, kind of like new," I admit to her and pull out the chair at the table, debating on what I should tell her. I want to spill everything, every last detail.

"Does he make you happy?" she asks.

"Yeah, happy but worried."

"But happy?" she asks again and I let out a short laugh, pulling one knee into my chest balancing my foot on the edge of the chair.

"Yeah, he really does make me happy. He makes me feel like me."

"It might take some time not to worry, you know?"

Swaying in my chair, I know she's right. I hate time, though, it hasn't been good to me.

"Yeah," I agree with her and then ask, "Want to take my mind off of it? Or is one a.m. a little too late and you'd rather sleep."

The sound of her rolling over in bed filters through the phone before she lets out an easy sigh. "I may have met a man," she says and then hums. I'm grateful for her, for friendship, for her stories. I try not to think about the fact that I probably won't see her very much once this is all said and done.

Instead I laugh along with her and decide I'm grateful phone calls exist.

It's not long after that I hang up, thanking her and telling her to have sweet dreams of her dark-haired mystery man that I hear their bikes.

Breathing in deep, I down the last of the decaf tea and head to the sink to wash out the cup. I grew up to that sound, the rev of the engines. I know it so well, I can clearly hear two of them.

I don't know what exactly is going on with the three of us, but I'm grateful both of them are coming home to me. Whatever it is we're doing, I want it. I want both of them however I can have them.

Reed comes in first, holding the door open for Cill. Adrenaline pushes me to move to the threshold and fuck I wish I hadn't. I'm paralyzed by the sight of Cillian. Tremors run up my spine.

He's covered in blood. His shirt is stained.

"Oh my God," I nearly fall to the floor, my trembling hands

covering my mouth. "Hey, Hellcat," he says. "It's not mine," he clarifies and although that's fucking horrible in and of itself, the relief is immediate.

"Are you all right?" I ask and look over both of them, still standing in the threshold and too scared to move. Reed closes the door and I note there's a bit of blood on him too that's smeared across his shirt.

"We're both fine." Reed adds, "Promise."

"What did you do?"

"We ended things here."

Things. I know exactly what that means. It's his uncle's blood.

"Do we need to leave?"

Cill nods, catching my eyes as he pulls the shirt over his head. "We'll pack up and move tonight.

"Tonight?" Surprise is evident in my rushed-out word.

Cill nods as if it's not a big deal to pick up and move in the middle of the night. "We're starting over. Just us, and Reed."

It takes me a minute to process what he's said, my head spins with all of this happening at once. "Reed too?"

"I think the three of us should keep doing what we are ..." Cill says and lets his gaze drift down my body. "What do you think, Reed?" He looks over his shoulder at Reed, who's stripping down to take off the bloodied clothes.

His muscles ripple as he does the same, looking me up and down like I'm some kind of meal for the two of them to enjoy together. He even licks his lower lip before nodding and saying, "I think that's exactly what I want."

My body flushes from head to toe. I can't believe he just said that. I can't believe that Cillian is standing in the middle of my kitchen with someone else's blood on him, and talking about sharing me with his best friend.

Something in my heart clicks into place. I meet Reed's deep brown eyes, feeling shy. I can't speak. I never dreamed that Cill would suggest something like this. I didn't think I'd want him to, but now that he has, I can't imagine it being any other way.

"You like that, don't you?" Cill questions.

I'm hesitant to nod, but I do it. "I just want to love you two." I swallow down every apprehension.

"Good," he says with finality. "'Cause that's all I want too."

"Same," Reed adds. "We love you, Kat."

I stare between the two of them, not believing while also eager for this to be true. "I love you both too."

Epilogue

Kat

One Week Later

Reed drives with the windows down and one arm out in the California breeze. It's taken us over a week to get here. We could have made the trip faster, but none of us wanted to. Their bikes are in the back and we got a notice that everything we packed up and shipped arrived at the new place.

We're almost there. I have no idea what it'll be like. But I know I'll have both Reed and Cillian, so I'll make it home.

I was content enough at the flower shop, but nothing compares to being on the open road with Reed and Cill. We find out-of-the-way motels that have been lovingly cared for by the owners and stay up all night in bed together. We stop at half of the roadside attractions on the way out west. We drive in the desert under the stars. We eat at diners that have menus the size of a phone book. Every single thing we ever talked about doing when we were young and dumb and thought life ahead of us was going to be an easy road, we do.

Our motto now is to live with no regrets and every day we accomplish that, I believe it more and more.

I have my feet sprawled across the back seat. Cill rides in the passenger seat. He's looking out the window at the scenery, his face relaxed.

Kat: We finally got to the coast!

Lydia: Took you long enough :D

Kat: There were lots of sights to see ;)

Kat: You should come out here with us. Everywhere we've been is absolutely gorgeous

Lydia: You trying to set me up with Reed?

I smile at the phone. I know she's joking, but I'm going to answer her honestly. It feels good to say it out loud. Or type it, I suppose.

Kat: No. I meant it when I told you I'm claiming both of them.

Kat: But I mean it. You should come out here

There's a silence, and I wonder if she's thinking of what to say. I told her we're a throuple the other day and she thought I was joking at first. I know it's not normal, but when the hell have our lives ever been normal? At this point, I'll settle with safe and content. I just want to be safe, and I am when I'm between them both.

Lydia: You gonna run forever?

Kat: We're not running. We're just … making a new start.

It's easy to hope with these two men.

A sign passes by on the side of the road.

"Reed," I call up. "Take the next exit."

"How come? We're not quite there yet."

"I want to see the ocean."

Cill turns around and smiles at me. "You want to look at something big and all-consuming, Hellcat? If you do, I have another idea."

"Take me to the ocean," I tell him, teasing. "And then you can show me how all-consuming you are."

He doesn't have to show me.

I already know.

CILL

I didn't just tell Finn that I sent the info to The Ruin, I didn't tell him shit and as far as I'm concerned, I don't owe it to him. I don't owe anything more to Cavanaugh Crest than I already gave. He'll make assumptions maybe, ask questions and possibly put the pieces together. But the old man will be fine without me. Just like he was for the four years I was away. The thing about prison is that you learn to keep your mouth shut, and I did. I spent four fucking years locked away. My best friend and the love of my life lived in hell, and my father was murdered.

But that's all over now. We're on the other side of the country, with sunny skies and an open road. Nobody out here knows what I did. Nobody's ever going to know, except the two people in the car with me. They're the only ones that matter.

A club can be a family, if you let it. But when push comes to shove, you learn who your real family is. My hellcat's mine. I'll spend the rest of my life giving her what she needs, which is both of us.

The ocean comes into view as we pull off the freeway. "There it is, Hellcat. The Pacific Ocean."

She leans up between the front seats to look. It's a sight to see. Something about all those waves in the sun. This is why I'll never tell her no.

"Is it everything you ever dreamed of?" I say, joking.

Kat turns her head and kisses my cheek. "I never dream of the ocean," she says. "All I ever dream about is you." She settles down, biting her bottom lip as she peeks at Reed, a blush creeping up her cheeks, "And you."

THIS "THE END"
comes with a *very sinful*
happily ever after

About the Author

Thank you so much for reading my romances. I'm just a stay at home Mom and an avid reader turned Author and I couldn't be happier.

I hope you love my books as much as I do!

More by Willow Winters
www.willowwinterswrites.com/books

Made in the USA
Las Vegas, NV
14 September 2023